HIGH NOON IN SNAKE RIDGE

Matthew Jennings returns to Snake Ridge to reconcile with his respectable family — and finds his brother lying dead. To track down the killer, he secures a position as deputy town marshal; but when he follows the evidence, it leads to a man who must be innocent: his own father. Even worse, a feuding outlaw gives him an ultimatum to leave town by noon, or die . . . Matthew's resolve to turn his back on his past will be tested to breaking point before he faces a high noon showdown.

Books by Scott Connor
in the Linford Western Library:

AMBUSH IN DUST CREEK
SIVER GULCH FEUD
GOLDEN SUNDOWN
CLEARWATER JUSTICE
ESCAPE FROM FORT BENTON
RETURN TO BLACK ROCK
LAST STAGE TO LONESOME
McGUIRE, MANHUNTER
RAIDERS OF THE MISSION SAN JUAN
COLTAINE'S REVENGE
STAND-OFF AT COPPER TOWN
SIEGE AT HOPE WELLS
THE SONS OF CASEY O'DONNELL
RIDE THE SAVAGE RIVER

SCOTT CONNOR

◆

HIGH NOON IN SNAKE RIDGE

Complete and Unabridged

LINFORD
Leicester

First published in Great Britain in 2012 by
Robert Hale Limited
London

First Linford Edition
published 2014
by arrangement with
Robert Hale Limited
London

A catalogue record for this book is available
from the British Library.

ISBN 978–1–4448–1992–2

Published by
F. A. Thorpe (Publishing)
Anstey, Leicestershire

Set by Words & Graphics Ltd.
Anstey, Leicestershire
Printed and bound in Great Britain by
T. J. International Ltd., Padstow, Cornwall

This book is printed on acid-free paper

1

'See you soon, Matthew,' the guard said with a smirk.

Matthew Jennings stayed silent while the gate of the Bozeman Point jail creaked open and presented him with an uninterrupted view of featureless plains that stretched to the impossibly far away horizon.

'I'm not coming back,' he said as the vastness drew him forward.

'They all say that.'

When Matthew didn't reply, the guard kicked his rump, making him drop to his knees. Matthew stared at the ground while concentrating on the fact that this would be the last time he'd be on the receiving end of such treatment.

He got to his feet, but the moment he turned around, a saddlebag slapped him in the face and wrapped around his

1

head. While the guard laughed, he struggled to extricate himself and, by the time he'd dragged the bag away, the gate was slamming shut.

Matthew glared at the closed gate, but the lure of the open space made him dismiss the thought of banging on it and shouting oaths at the guard.

He turned and stared at the endless nothing, deciding he'd never get bored of solitude, of not being given orders, of not being locked up in a small space.

He must have stood there for a while as, when he directed his thoughts to his next actions, the sun was warming his back, having risen above the clouds after his sunup release.

Firstly, he investigated what was in the bag. It didn't take long. It was empty.

Ten years of incarceration had taken away the memory of what possessions he'd had when he'd been locked away, but he doubted there'd been much.

He dropped the bag to the ground and turned north towards the town of

Bozeman Point. At a steady pace, he embarked on the ten-mile walk.

He was still revelling in the simple pleasures of having the sun on his back and the wind in his hair when he walked into town. He located the station where he found out that the train was due in an hour.

As he reckoned that nobody would complain if he rode the rails, he leaned back against the station house wall in a position that kept him apart from the other congregating passengers — not that anyone came close to him.

When the train arrived, he noted two freight cars at the back and so he made his slow way towards them. He watched out for anyone paying him undue attention, but, as it turned out, he wasn't the only one planning to take this uncomfortable option.

A man emerged from behind the station house and, with his head down, ran to the freight cars. Without checking that anyone was watching him, he slid open the first door, peered around, and then moved on to the second car where he clambered inside quickly.

Matthew reckoned that moving quickly was the right way to act and so he hurried to the open door. When he reached it, two arms were thrust down. He locked hands and let the man draw him up.

'Howdy, Matthew,' his helper said. His voice was deep and familiar. 'It's been a while.'

In the otherwise empty car, Matthew sat back against the wall where he could see outside through the space left by a missing plank. As his eyes accustomed to the lower light level inside, with a start he confirmed his companion's identity.

'Creighton Kendrick,' Matthew said, a smile breaking out now that he'd enjoyed his first break since leaving jail. 'Was this a coincidence or were you waiting for me?'

'I'd already decided to head west.' Creighton slid the door closed cutting down the light level to just the thin strips of daylight that sliced through the gaps in the planks, and then settled down in a corner of the car. 'But I thought I'd wait and ride along with you.'

His reply had been reasonable, but it still gave Matthew an uneasy feeling.

'I'm obliged for the company,' he said, having decided to mention the debt Creighton owed him. 'After all, I haven't seen my old friend for many years.'

'I'm grateful you never told anyone about me. So I've decided to cut you in on what you're owed.' Creighton glanced through the gaps in the wood, presumably to confirm that nobody was close. 'That's a half share in four thousand dollars.'

'I'm surprised any of it's left,' Matthew said, feeling pleased that the possibility didn't excite him. When Creighton only smiled, he hazarded a guess. 'I assume that means the others are dead.'

'Nope. After they caught you, Elijah

double-crossed us and stole our money. Then Tarrant and me got detained for a while on another matter, so we had to postpone the chase.'

Matthew frowned, acknowledging the hardships they'd suffered.

'Is Tarrant out yet?'

'He should be, but I couldn't find him. I did find Elijah. He returned to Snake Ridge and used our money to buy respect. Some say he could be the next town mayor.'

Matthew's first day outside jail had already tired him and so this revelation didn't surprise him as much as the incredulous expression that Creighton provided, suggesting it should.

'Elijah was a single-minded man. I wish him luck.'

'I sure don't.'

Matthew considered Creighton's frown and gathered an inkling of the full story. As the train lurched into motion, he raised his voice to be heard over the growing clamour of the rattling cars and screeching wheels.

'You've already tried and failed to get the money off him.'

'Three months ago I saw his picture.' Creighton withdrew a battered sheet of paper from his pocket. He tossed it on the floor and it fell open to show that it was the *Snake Ridge Gazette*. 'I offered him a deal to keep quiet about his past, but he called my bluff and had me run out of town. I've not got close to him since, but I reckon you'll do better.'

Matthew shook his head. 'I'm going back to my hometown, but I'm not going back to my old ways. He can keep my share of the money. You want your share back, settle it with him.'

'I'd wondered if jail might have changed you.' Creighton's benign expression flicked to a snarl in a moment as he drew his six-shooter. 'It's eighty miles to the next town. If I dump your body out of the train, nobody will ever find it.'

Creighton aimed the gun at a point above Matthew's head. He mouthed a count down from three. Then he fired.

The gunshot was deafening and even though Matthew knew Creighton had aimed high, he ducked. Then he glanced at the hole in the wall, judging that the slug had hit nine inches above his right ear.

When he looked at Creighton, he was now aiming nine inches lower.

'I'm not interested, old friend,' Matthew said, meeting Creighton's firm gaze.

Creighton narrowed his eyes with a look that said that despite the debt he owed him, he would shoot. But instead, he kicked the paper across the car.

'You should look at this first,' he said with a low voice. 'You know the current mayor, the man who'll be Elijah's main rival.'

Matthew picked up the paper and considered a picture depicting a line of men standing proudly before a locomotive. At the end was Elijah wearing a stove hat with a foot raised on to a wheel.

The text explained the momentous

event that was being celebrated, but Matthew didn't read it.

His gaze had centred on the man standing beside Elijah, the only other man in the picture he recognized. He refolded the page and threw it back to Creighton.

'I'll do what I can,' he said.

2

'You have a visitor, Mr Jennings,' Wilson Coney said with a hushed tone as he peered in through the office door.

'Tell him to go away,' a strident voice said from inside the office.

Wilson turned to Matthew while closing the door behind his back.

'He's too busy to see you.' He offered an ingratiating smile. 'Would you like to make an appointment?'

'I'd be obliged,' Matthew said using a deferential tone.

He was beckoned to Wilson's desk and the official rummaged around for an appointment book. But the moment he turned his back on him, Matthew headed to the door.

To Matthew's surprise, his brother wasn't inside. Instead, his father Granville, a thin, steel-haired man with round spectacles perched on the end of his nose, was sitting behind a desk. Only his head was visible behind the desk that was covered with so much paperwork, it made him appear as busy as Wilson had claimed.

Wilson put a hand on Matthew's shoulder and tugged, but the small man couldn't move him and so he slipped into the doorway beside him.

'I'm sorry,' he whined, wringing his hands. 'He ignored me.'

Granville didn't reply or even look up from the document he was reading, and so Matthew took a long pace forward.

'I reckoned,' he said, 'you wouldn't be too busy to see your son.'

Granville flinched before he got himself under control with a roll of the shoulders. Then, with a hand to his brow, he finished the section he was reading.

'You were wrong,' he said, looking up over the top of his glasses to see him for the first time in over ten years.

To avoid his piercing gaze, Matthew

walked around gesturing at the ornate office.

'I'm pleased you've done well.'

'This is your brother's office, and I'm proud to be his assistant.' Granville pursed his lips and the silence let Matthew fill in the detail for himself — that he wasn't proud of him. 'But that's no concern of yours.'

'It is,' Matthew said, struggling to find an appropriate response. 'I'm interested in what my family has been doing.'

'I've never been interested in your activities.' Granville looked down and read a few lines, but the strain of ignoring Matthew made him crease his brow and so, with an angry gesture, he pushed the document aside. 'But I knew they'd let you out.'

Matthew sighed, pleased that he'd broached the difficult subject. He took a deep breath before delivering the speech he'd rehearsed beforehand.

'Spending ten years in prison was enough for me. I want to change my life, but people take one look at me and work out where I've been. I thought my family might treat me differently.'

Granville had been nodding, but the final request made him raise an eyebrow. Then, with a snort of irritation, he withdrew bills from his pocket and deposited them onto the top of a pile of papers.

'There's thirty dollars here,' he said, gesturing at the money. 'That should be enough to get rid of you.'

'Obliged, but I meant I was looking for work. My brother was always good to me and I enjoyed his company.' Matthew paused, this time letting his father fill in the unsaid detail for himself. 'I intend to stay here and renew our friendship. So I'll need work to pay my way.'

Granville treated him to two raised eyebrows. Then he considered him with his hands raised and the fingertips touching in an attitude of prayer.

'Take the money and go.' Granville fanned out the bills. 'I don't want you around reminding everyone that I still have you for a son.'

Matthew walked up to the desk and picked up the bills. He flicked through them, confirming that his father had been as generous as he had claimed. Then with a sneer he hurled the money at him, making him jerk away.

'I need money real bad,' Matthew snapped as the bills fluttered to the floor, 'but not that badly.'

Then, with as much dignity as he could muster, he turned on his heel and left the office. He was halfway down the stairs when Granville started berating Wilson for having let him in.

Down in the lobby, Matthew took deep breaths to calm himself down. When that didn't work, he looked through a window at the bustling town and tried to enjoy the everyday — for others — sight of people going about their business.

Since he'd left, Snake Ridge had expanded. A railroad bridge had been built ten miles out of town across what had once been deemed an impassable gorge. Then a depot had been built, which had attracted yet more people. A small settlement that twenty years ago had only one trading post now had a hundred times more businesses.

He opened the door and, aside from the wood creaking, a low noise sounded. Matthew stopped and the sound came again, this time letting him identify it as someone groaning.

He ducked outside, confirmed that nobody was close by, and then slipped back into the lobby. His gaze quickly centred on the closed door at the bottom of the stairs.

He hurried to the room and cautiously put a hand to the wood. The door swung open to reveal a table and a line of chairs around the walls. One of the chairs had been toppled and that drew his attention to the feet sticking out beyond the table in the far corner.

At a run he rounded the table and

then, when he saw the blood, he skidded to a halt. He hadn't seen his brother Newman in ten years, but he recognized the wounded man's sparse fair hair and his tall form.

Newman was lying on his chest. The volume of blood that had pooled beneath him suggested that he'd been hurt some time ago, perhaps even before Matthew had arrived.

Meeting Newman had been the only part of his homecoming he'd been looking forward to. So the sight of him lying there, apparently stabbed and possibly dying, made Matthew sway and he had to grab the table to stop himself falling over.

With a heavy heart, Matthew turned him over, and his brother flopped on to his back to stare upwards with blank eyes.

'Who did this?' Matthew murmured, aghast as he considered his blood-soaked chest.

Newman twitched and he gasped in a ragged breath. His eyes moved and his unfocused gaze drifted to Matthew and then past him.

'Matthew?' Newman whispered, his voice like the wind. 'Is that really you?'

'It is. I've come back.' Matthew looked at the door. 'And I need to get you to help.'

'There's so much I want to tell you, but it's too late.' Newman exhaled a long breath. 'I forgive you.'

Then his head lolled to the side. When he didn't draw in another breath, Matthew ran from the room calling for the help that he knew his brother was already beyond needing.

⋆ ⋆ ⋆

Matthew's former partner in crime, Elijah Moon, owned the Horned Moon. As the saloon looked lowly enough to eke out his meagre funds, Matthew went in and bustled to the bar.

Creighton had given him enough money for a room along with a few drinks, so he leaned on the counter beside a sour-faced man who was drinking himself into oblivion. Matthew reckoned he'd found the right place to spend a couple of hours and, with an equally sour expression, he ordered a drink and revelled in the sullen atmosphere.

Nobody talked to him and only a low susurration of muttered conversations filled the room, letting him put his thoughts in order about his past so that he could plan his future.

Ten years ago, in what now felt like it had been a different life, he had lived here. While his elder brother Newman had been responsible, he'd been wayward. His only memories of his family came from the time after his mother's death, when he had argued with his father while Newman leapt to his defence.

He'd met three equally disillusioned young men, who had just ridden into town. With Elijah Moon, Tarrant Blocker and Creighton Kendrick he had spirited away the contents of his hometown's bank in the dead of night.

The robbery had gone so smoothly, the finger of suspicion had never been pointed at them. This had especially pleased him, as his brother had just delighted his father by being appointed as the town's first marshal.

A month later, when they'd split up the $4,000 they'd hidden away, the money no longer felt substantial and the urge to steal again had consumed them. They'd moved on, hoping to continue their success.

Creighton had been the leader, planning their activities in meticulous detail. Tarrant had been the safe-breaker, priding himself that no lock could defeat his light fingers. Elijah had been the gunman, although Creighton's planning had been so good his talent hadn't been used.

When he thought back, Matthew had to admit his role had been the least skilled. He had gone into town

19

first, looked over the area, and reported back. His had been the only face anyone saw and that had been his downfall.

After a month of planning, their first raid after leaving Snake Ridge had gone disastrously wrong.

The bank staff in Rock Pass had been edgy and his activities had aroused suspicion, so before the other three men had ridden into town, law officers had descended on him. While the others melted away, he'd been arrested for attempted bank robbery, the only charge against him that could be proven.

He'd kept his silence about the others' involvement. But he'd still got ten years.

The only positive result was that his time in jail had convinced him that he wouldn't return to his old ways, but his homecoming had been even more disastrous than he'd feared.

That thought made him grip his glass tightly and so confirm he did want one thing: to see Newman's killer brought to justice.

Sundown arrived and he was just thinking about seeking out a room when a raised voice sounded behind him. He hunched over his drink and ignored the distraction, but the drinker to his left, Walt, screeched and then was dragged backwards and deposited on the floor with a thud.

Laughter filled the saloon as the inebriated man sprawled around like a beached fish. Two men, identified by the other customers' murmured comments as being the Deno brothers, Abraham and Lawrence, took up his position at the bar.

'You'd be Matthew Jennings,' Abraham said with a grin. 'Elijah saw you. We're here to give you your first and only warning.'

Matthew cradled his drink against his chest and leaned back against the bar. The brothers were the kind of arrogant and surly men he'd met often in prison, men who rose up through the prison hierarchy quickly or, equally as quickly ended up dead.

'I'm enjoying my whiskey in peace,' Matthew said with a low tone. He raised a glass that contained only dregs.

Abraham appraised him. 'So enjoy it. Then move on. Snake Ridge's not your kind of town no more.'

'If only you hadn't said that,' Matthew murmured, anger rising from deep in his belly as another man took the same attitude as his father had.

On the floor, Walt crawled away making Abraham glance at him. Matthew seized that moment as his best to act and he threw his glass at Abraham.

He had hoped to hit his face, but his hurried action was aimed poorly and the glass only bounced off his chest before dropping to the floor. His response still took Abraham by surprise and he raised a hand in a warding off gesture that was too slow to stop Matthew pushing away from the bar and aiming a running punch at him.

The swirling blow struck Abraham's

cheek, knocking his head down, but he kept his hand raised and so Matthew grabbed his wrist and then twisted while moving behind him. He finished up with his opponent's wrist held in the middle of his back while he wrapped his other arm around his neck to hold him securely.

'Get off me,' Abraham grunted.

'I will,' Matthew said calmly, 'if you help my friend back to the bar and buy us both a drink.'

A customer drew in his breath and other customers registered their surprise that he'd stood up to the brothers. When Lawrence moved closer, he raised his opponent's arm making him grunt and then twist as he sought to throw him aside, but Matthew stood his ground.

'Do as he says,' Abraham said to his brother when he failed to dislodge him. 'Prop Walt up against the bar.'

Lawrence glared at Matthew. Then, with a mocking show of being helpful to limit the indignity of being ordered about, he carefully helped Walt to his feet and deposited him against the bar.

Walt wasted no time in gathering up his whiskey bottle with a shaking hand and pouring himself a measure.

'Obliged,' Matthew said into his opponent's ear.

'Enjoy the rest of the evening.'

He pushed Abraham away. When both men were facing him, he treated them to a smile and then backed away for a pace.

'You not staying to have your final drink with us?' Abraham said, flexing his elbow.

'No,' Matthew said, eyeing both men's sneers. He turned away before Abraham could provide what would surely be another threat, but he didn't move off. 'Maybe another night, with Elijah.'

With the brothers' gazes burning into his neck, Matthew walked to the door. Outside he speeded up to a brisk walk while casting glances over his shoulder, but they didn't follow him out.

★ ★ ★

Creighton had jumped off the train five miles out of town, after which he'd planned to hole up at Hunter's Pass to await news about Matthew's trip into Snake Ridge. As he had more important things to consider than his feud, Matthew dismissed seeing him again for now.

He picked the hotel he would stay in, the dingy and sour-smelling Hotel Moonshine, and paid a dollar for a room for the night. Then he sat in a chair in the lobby where he could see through the grimy window and down the road to the Horned Moon.

As he expected, twenty minutes later Abraham and Lawrence came out. They headed towards the hotel, making Matthew tense, but they walked by, only a change in pace hinting that they knew he was here. As soon as they'd disappeared into the dark, Matthew went to his room.

He lay on his sagging and unmade

bed fully clothed staring at a mildew patch on the ceiling. When his imagination let him see the misshapen blob as a map of the town, he used it to help him plan where he would look for work.

Sadly, his mind kept returning to Newman and his unknown killer. So he had yet to come up with any plans for the next day when someone knocked on the door.

He was unarmed so he limited himself to moving his weight so that he could get up quickly. He bade the man to enter.

'You busy, Matthew?' Marshal Bob Wyndham said when the door had swung open.

Matthew lowered his gaze to meet lively blue eyes and a firm jaw.

'Nope,' Matthew said. 'And I've not remembered anything else about what I saw in the mayor's office.'

'It's not about that. I heard that earlier tonight you launched an unprovoked attack on two defenceless men in the Horned Moon.'

'I guess I did,' Matthew said with a sigh. 'What are you planning to do about it?'

The lawman smiled. 'I'm planning to offer you a job.'

3

'You want to appoint me as your deputy town marshal?' Matthew spluttered.

He sat on the edge of his bed and waited for Wyndham to explain his joke. But the lawman maintained his stern expression as he sat on the chair beside the door.

'Sure do,' he said in a sombre tone. 'You're the first man who's impressed me.'

'I may be a Jennings, but I'm not my brother.' Matthew spread his arms inviting him to look him up and down.

'You're clearly down on your luck, but I reckon you're looking for honest work for fair pay.' Wyndham frowned. 'And you stood up to Elijah Moon's men when they were looking for trouble.'

Matthew winced and then got up quickly so the lawman wouldn't detect that his behaviour hadn't been quite as selfless as he thought.

'Hopefully they didn't harm Walt afterwards.'

'Sadly, they did. Now they're cooling off in a cell.'

Matthew went to the window, now feeling irritated that he'd walked away from the confrontation.

He could see over the tops of several low buildings to the mayor's office where a light still burned. He imagined his father's annoyance if he were to find out that his wayward son had followed his responsible son's lead in serving Snake Ridge in an official capacity.

Then his gaze drifted down to the mercantile opposite the hotel. With a sudden understanding of the town's layout, he realized that a bank had once stood there. A woman he'd been fond of, Abigail Summers, had worked there as a teller, but then the lure of money had made him abuse her trust.

Feeling ashamed, he turned away and shook his head.

'I'm obliged for your offer and I'm mighty tempted, but I'm not the right man to be your deputy.'

Wyndham slapped his legs and stood up.

'Sleep on that decision. See me in the morning if you change your mind.'

Wyndham tipped his hat and then left, leaving Matthew to turn back to the window. He was still there thirty minutes later when the light went off in the mayor's office.

So, with a sigh, he looked over the town. Lights still burned in the many saloons on this side of town from where sounds of revelry reached him, but he'd chosen his hotel well as it was several buildings away from the noise.

The only sign of life nearby was the light cast by a smoker who was standing in the shadows outside the mercantile. But when Matthew decided that the man was looking at him, the light dropped to the ground and was extinguished by a boot. The man then melted into the gloom.

Matthew retired to his bed, but he couldn't dismiss the uneasy feeling that he was being watched.

The next morning he still felt edgy, so he went straight to the law office. He noted the Wanted posters outside.

The newest poster featured the blank face of Mayor Newman Jennings' killer. A stuck-on banner promised that a significant bounty would be announced soon.

The thought hit him that as a lawman he could help with the search for his brother's killer. His heart quickened. But like last night, he shook the idea away. The marshal would surely sack him the moment he found out that he was fresh out of jail.

'Matthew,' a woman said, 'is that you?'

Matthew swirled round to face the woman he'd thought about the night before, but who he'd tried not to think about during his ten years of incarceration.

'Abigail Summers,' he said. 'You're

looking mighty fine.'

He wasn't kidding, as even her anger-reddened face couldn't mask the pleasing twinkle in her eyes.

'I'm Abigail Summers no longer,' she declared, 'and you're not looking fine. Jail's destroyed you, not that there was anything worth keeping in the first place.'

He ventured a smile. 'There used to be enough to interest you.'

That proved to be the worst thing he could have said, as she took a long pace forward and then looked him up and down with unconcealed disgust.

'If there's even a grain of decency left in your rancid hide, you'll leave town and never return so I don't have to think about how low I fell.'

Then she did the one thing that his hasty departure from town ten years ago had let him avoid: she slapped his right cheek with a stinging blow. And, when he shook off the blow, she slapped his left cheek even harder bending him double. Then, for good measure, she kicked his ankle.

He hopped on the spot while her heels clicked down the boardwalk. Then, with a glance at her receding form, he headed into the law office.

'Marshal Wyndham,' he said, still fingering a smarting cheek, 'I reckon it's time I made amends.'

'Obliged you changed your mind,' Wyndham said, getting up from behind his desk to shake his hand.

'Where do I start?'

'I was about to leave to escort Bodie Sanborn into town. He's coming from Red Town with the bounty Franklin Buxton's posting for finding the mayor's killer. Now you can go in my place.'

'Who's likely to be the new mayor?' Matthew asked after Wyndham had given him details of Bodie's route.

Wyndham returned to his desk and cast him a wide smile.

'I'll enjoy working with a man who thinks in the same way as I do. Who had the most to gain from Newman's death is the first question I considered.'

In reality, Matthew had been wondering if his father might stand, but with Wyndham assuming he was thinking like a lawman, he responded appropriately.

'I'd guess that's Elijah Moon.'

'You'd guess right.' Wyndham gestured at the window, indicating the town. 'Elijah owns the saloons, gambling haunts, and hotels on the far side of town. They cater for the lowest dregs and so they attract the most trouble. I reckon he was involved, except I can't prove nothing.'

'Will anyone else stand?' Matthew asked levelly.

'The declarations have to be in by noon in two days, but it looks as if it'll be a battle between Elijah and your father. Thankfully, Granville has the backing of Franklin Buxton, Elijah's business rival, along with the sentiment.'

Matthew sighed, as the enormity of the task of living up to his family's reputation hit him.

'Sentiment,' he said, 'isn't a word I'd associate with my father.'

* * *

Ten miles out of town, Matthew stopped before the bridge. As it towered above the winding blue ribbon of the river, he considered how he would deal with the short, but nerve-jangling trip across Snake Gorge.

The bridge was narrow, providing room for just the railroad tracks and one rider to ride on either side. Thick timber railings gave comfort to anyone making the crossing, but the rails were twenty feet apart and it would be easy to slip between them after which there was nothing below but the river and the rocky sides.

He was relieved to see a rider heading down on to the bridge on the other side. He was too far away for him to work out if he matched Bodie Sanborn's description, but he waited to avoid spooking the horse on a crossing that would require the rider's full concentration.

The rider set his gaze on the end of the bridge as he rode on at a walking pace. The man was halfway across when a loud crack tore out, the sound echoing in the gorge.

Matthew looked down, thinking that there was a problem with the bridge. Then the crack came again and this time he recognized it as gunfire.

The rider scrambled for his six-shooter while keeping his horse on a tight rein. His gaze picked out Matthew.

'It wasn't me,' Matthew shouted, raising a hand. 'I'm Deputy Matthew Jennings.'

'Obliged you came to meet me,' the man said, confirming his identity.

Then he trained his gun on the other side of the gorge. He fired two rapid shots and then moved on at a faster pace.

He covered half the remaining distance to the end of the bridge, but then Matthew saw movement on the other side of the gorge close to where Bodie had aimed. Matthew gestured at the spot.

Bodie looked over his shoulder, but then stood up straight with his back arched. A gunshot sounded a moment later as he slid from the saddle.

Bodie waved his arms to try to still his progress, but he succeeded only in dislodging his saddlebag and dragging it down with him. He collapsed on to the bridge and came to rest closer to the edge than to the railroad tracks while his horse skittered off along the tracks.

Matthew dismounted and edged on to the bridge. With his gun drawn, he embarked on quick journeys between the rails where he paused for differing lengths of time, but the gunman didn't appear and he reached the wounded man without mishap.

Bodie was lying on his back with his gun hand held across his chest. Blood was seeping out from under him and dribbling along the planks.

He murmured something, but his voice was too weak for Matthew to hear the words. Then he arched his back and wheezed out a long breath.

Matthew patted his shoulder. Then, bent double, he moved over to the edge of the bridge where he saw a flash of colour as the gunman moved position.

Matthew hunkered down and loosed off two quick shots that made puffs of dust rise up from rocks ten feet below the gunman, but they were close enough to make him scurry back into hiding.

For the next five minutes Matthew waited for him to act. When the shooter stayed down, he crawled away to check on Bodie, but he was still and he didn't react when Matthew slapped his cheek.

Judging that a rail shielded him from the gunman, Matthew shuffled over to the saddlebag and swung open the flap. Wads of bills filled the bag.

The sight of the money didn't excite him as it once would have and so he swung the flap back. With the bag tucked under an arm, he hurried to a rail.

The shooter wasn't visible, so he repeated the method he'd used to come on to the bridge by running and pausing at the rails.

No gunfire sounded on the return journey. Back on firm ground, he hid behind the corner post where he reckoned he could defend himself indefinitely against a gunman who would have to take risks to approach him.

He waited for that attack, but aside from the horse mooching around on the tracks and the trailing end of Bodie's jacket blowing in the breeze, Matthew saw no movement.

'So you've got your thieving hands on a lot of money again, Matthew,' the gunman shouted unexpectedly from the other side of the gorge.

'You'll never get it,' Matthew shouted, trying to work out where the gunman was hiding. 'And how do you know me?'

'I could never forget you, but I never expected to see you again. Then there you were roaming around town, getting into a fight, talking with Marshal Wyndham.'

'So you were the man standing outside the mercantile last night. What do you want from me?'

'I'll let you figure that out. Then I'll kill you.'

Gunfire tore into the post, making Matthew jerk away. He waited until the volley died out and then moved into the open, but the man didn't show again.

4

'I wouldn't have believed it if I hadn't seen it with my own eyes,' Elijah Moon said, standing in the law office doorway with his hands on his hips. 'Matthew Jennings has returned with a death wish.'

Matthew leaned back in his chair to display the badge that he was already proud of. Earlier, Wyndham had left to deliver the bounty to Franklin, after which he'd headed to the bridge, leaving Matthew to write his report on the incident.

He had enjoyed the work and so even Elijah's presence couldn't stifle his contented mood.

'That's Deputy Matthew Jennings to you, a legally sworn in officer of the law in Snake Ridge.'

Elijah came across the office and placed his hands on Matthew's desk while leaning forward to glare at him.

'So you're now protecting the same people who lost money in the bank raid ten years ago,' Elijah snorted. 'One word from me about that and your life will be short and painful.'

Matthew couldn't help but laugh. 'You're talking about the bank robbery we carried out together.'

Elijah sneered. 'While you've been breaking rocks, I've been good to this town. If you accuse me, who do you think people will believe?'

Matthew met Elijah's icy gaze. 'The thing is, you wasted your breath with that threat. I want to start a new life and that means I don't want your dirty money.'

Elijah stood up straight, his right eye twitching as he failed to hide his anger. He slammed a fist on the desk sending his brother's poster, amended with the bounty details, fluttering to the floor.

'A lowlife from my past doesn't tell me what to do just because the marshal thought it'd be funny to pin him to a badge.'

Matthew rescued the poster and rolled it up carefully so that Elijah could see its legend, but he didn't detect that it discomforted him.

'And a lowlife from my past doesn't tell me what to do just because he built an empire with money stolen from decent folk.'

Elijah stepped back from the desk. 'Leave. There's nothing for you here. Your brother's dead, your father hates you, and if you think Abigail will take you back, you're more foolish than you look.'

'I've already spoken with Granville and Abigail.'

Elijah snorted a disbelieving laugh and then gestured at the door to the jailhouse in which the Deno brothers were residing.

'Now release my men.'

Matthew locked his hands behind his head with a show of being relaxed.

'Quit with the demands. They don't leave here on your orders, or mine for that matter.'

Elijah pointed a firm finger at him. 'That's the last time you defy me. Now I'm — '

'You weren't listening.' Matthew glanced at the clock on the wall behind Elijah. It was five past noon. 'Marshal Wyndham told me to release them at noon. If you and I hadn't been enjoying this pleasant conversation, they'd already be free.'

While Elijah muttered to himself, Matthew went into the adjoining jailhouse. Wyndham must have informed the prisoners of his change in status, as they didn't register surprise.

Instead, they cast him surly glares as they shuffled away. Then, when Elijah saw them, he berated them for their stupidity in getting arrested. As Matthew returned to his desk, the brothers were hurrying outside, but Elijah stayed.

'You have until noon tomorrow to leave,' he said. 'Or what will happen to you will make your time in jail feel like a picnic.'

'I've been appointed to help find my

brother's killer,' Matthew said. 'I'm going nowhere until I find him.'

Matthew looked Elijah up and down with a gesture that said he'd already done that. Elijah responded with a sneer, then turned and left.

Despite the threats, Matthew whistled a merry tune as he cleaned out the jailhouse.

Later, when Wyndham returned having failed to find any tracks left by Bodie's killer, he joined him on a patrol around town.

At the corner of the block where he could see the mayor's office, he wondered when his father would hear about his new position and what his reaction would be. He entertained the thought that he would be impressed.

Then they moved on past Franklin Buxton's largest hotel, the Hotel Splendour. Matthew peered through the window expecting to see a genteel atmosphere, but instead the activity was of the kind he'd expect to see in the Hotel Moonshine.

People were scurrying about and a circle of men was engaged in a furious argument. Franklin was directing the chaos with arms waving and frantic orders.

'Silence!' Wyndham called when they'd headed inside. Within moments the hubbub quietened.

'It's terrible news,' Franklin said. He cast an angry glare around. 'The bounty's been stolen.'

Wyndham nodded. Then he paced around the room looking the staff up and down with a mixture of authority and suspicion before turning to Matthew.

'Guard the front door and make sure nobody leaves,' he said, 'while I start the questioning.'

Wyndham then led Franklin away to another room along with the nearest member of staff. With the boss gone, the staff stopped panicking and returned to carrying out their duties.

Matthew's duty became uncomfortable when the desk clerk returned to the lobby. He tried to avoid her eye, but she leaned on the counter and glared at him.

'Clearly,' Abigail said, 'you haven't got a grain of decency left in your rancid hide, after all.'

Matthew confirmed that nobody was showing an inclination to leave the hotel and then headed across the lobby.

'I stayed because I was offered a job.'

'I assume that means Marshal Wyndham doesn't know you were a jailbird.'

Matthew had expected that taunt and he avoided looking worried.

'He prefers to judge a man by his actions.'

'So do I.'

She busied herself with moving the reception book and other items around the counter. Matthew let her have the last word and was about to turn away when an obvious thought hit him.

Wyndham had followed Franklin's lead in questioning the staff, but they weren't the only people in the hotel. With no expectation that he would recognize any names, he turned the reception book around and started reading.

'Take your hands off that,' Abigail said, slapping his hand. 'These are valued guests and Franklin wouldn't want them disturbed.'

Matthew ignored her demand. The book detailed the guests' comings and goings. In the early afternoon only one man was in residence, and his was a familiar name. Matthew blinked back his surprise and then considered her, a smile on his face.

She returned his gaze, but then scuffing footfalls sounded and a lanky boy shuffled in from a back room. She shooed the boy away, but when he looked at Matthew, she left the counter to speak with him.

Once her back was turned to him, Matthew headed to the stairs. He took them two at a time while behind him, Abigail returned to the counter and demanded that he come back. When that failed to halt him, she hurried off shouting for Franklin's help.

A sign on the first floor directed him to room seven, so he wasted no time in heading down the corridor and then throwing open the door.

Inside, a man was sitting at the window looking outside. He turned to consider Matthew with no sign of surprise.

'Tarrant Blocker,' Matthew said, before re-using the words with which he'd welcomed Creighton Kendrick, the other member of their outlaw gang: 'Was this a coincidence or were you waiting for me?'

'Coincidence,' Tarrant said. 'And from the look of that star on your chest, you've had more luck than I've had.'

'I'm a lawman now,' Matthew said, 'and two thousand dollars has been stolen while sitting up here is a man with light fingers and poor aim.'

Tarrant gulped, his confused expression suggesting that he wasn't the man who had ambushed Bodie on the bridge.

'I'm not interested in Franklin's money. I'm only interested in Elijah Moon, the man who stole our money.'

Matthew nodded. 'Creighton is holed up at Hunter's Pass. Join up with him if you want, but I've moved on and I intend to do this job properly.'

'Except when the job involves a matter where you're personally involved, of course.'

Amongst his many problems, this was one of Matthew's biggest concerns, but approaching footfalls sounded in the corridor and so he spoke quickly.

'If Elijah killed my brother, I'll bring him to justice. But if you want to get back at him, do it discreetly and without me.'

Tarrant narrowed his eyes, but he accepted with a nod the line Matthew had drawn a moment before Franklin arrived with Wyndham at his shoulder. Abigail hadn't come with them.

'Get your deputy out of there, Wyndham,' Franklin said. 'His mistake could make this an even more costly day for me.'

'I will,' Wyndham said. 'But only after he's explained himself.'

Wyndham gave Matthew a stern look that told him to make his explanation a good one.

'Franklin assumed someone who worked for him stole the bounty,' Matthew said, sticking to the facts, 'but I wondered if it was a guest.'

Wyndham considered Tarrant and then the room, presumably wondering where he could have stashed the money. He shook his head and then beckoned Matthew to the door.

'This matter ends here,' he said.

Franklin barged past Matthew. While he launched into an apology, Matthew left and didn't speak until he and Wyndham stopped at the top of the stairs. In the lobby, Abigail was lurking around, but when she saw them, she slipped behind the counter.

'The staff wouldn't dare defy Franklin,' Matthew said, 'so someone else did it.'

'That's fine reasoning,' Wyndham said, 'but it's not fine enough to disobey my order to guard the front door.'

'But the money's long gone and besides, the back door's unguarded.'

'I took over as Snake Ridge's marshal from your brother last year,' Wyndham said, his calm tone more troubling than Franklin's ire. 'Like Newman before me, early on I made mistakes. I learnt from them. Now I'm a respected lawman. If you want to last in this job for long enough to learn from your mistakes, choose your next words carefully.'

'You're the boss,' Matthew said with a resigned tone. 'I'll only do what you tell me to do.'

'Then that mistake was worth making.'

While Wyndham moved on to resume his questioning, Matthew stood by the front door where Abigail glared at him over the counter with an eager expression that said she knew he'd erred.

When Franklin came downstairs, he stopped at the reception desk and spoke with Abigail in a surprisingly soft voice, making her fluff her hair with an embarrassed gesture.

Then the boy Matthew had seen earlier appeared and Franklin ruffled his fair hair while Abigail looked on and smiled. With a nod to himself, Matthew accepted she was more than Franklin's desk clerk.

'Is it over now, Pa?' the boy asked.

'The money's still missing, Jimmy,' Franklin said. He bent down although the boy was nearly his height. 'But there's nothing we can do now other than to wait for the lawmen to find the thief. So you can stop looking after your ma and help me.'

The boy beamed and, after hugging Abigail, joined Franklin in heading on to another room. Abigail watched them go but, when she turned away, her smile died. To avoid her gaze, Matthew looked at Franklin and Jimmy.

As they disappeared from view, he noted that Jimmy was acting maturely, as befitted a boy who was being groomed to take responsibility, and that he was tall for his age. Then the alternate interpretation hit him that Jimmy might not be bigger than he'd expect the child of a small man to be.

He flinched and looked at Abigail, who raised a hand, but before she could admonish him, a breathless Wyndham hurried into the lobby.

'Hurry, Matthew,' he demanded. 'We've got him.'

Matthew tore his gaze away from Abigail and joined Wyndham. Together they slipped outside and hurried down the boardwalk. While they ran, Matthew looked around animatedly to stop himself thinking about what Abigail clearly didn't want him to think about.

'Where did he go?' he asked when they reached the end of the road. His voice was hoarse, and not just from the exertion.

'I left the back door seemingly unguarded and the thief took the bait.' Wyndham pointed. 'He was followed until he slipped through a window in the mayor's office.'

Wyndham set off across the road and the surprising answer made Matthew dally before he broke into a run. At the office, Wyndham signalled the open window at the side of the building before he went through the main door.

The window led into the unoccupied waiting room where Matthew had found Newman. This fact made both men pause before they checked the downstairs rooms. Then they headed to the stairs.

Matthew tramped on behind Wyndham, feeling unready to see his father again, but the obsequious assistant Wilson Coney wasn't on duty and the door to the main office was open.

They stood in the doorway, listening, but Matthew heard nothing and the building had the cold feeling of being unoccupied.

'Is it usual,' Matthew said, 'for nobody to be here at this time of the day?'

'It isn't. Usually — ' Wyndham broke

off and then pointed at a second door.

Matthew nodded and so they paced quietly across the office to stand on either side of the door. In the other room, someone was moving about and so cautiously, Wyndham backhanded the door open to reveal Granville standing at the window.

He registered only slowly that the door had opened. Then he turned to reveal the saddlebag he clutched to his chest. He considered Matthew with a sneer.

'I heard you'd appointed a deputy, Wyndham,' he said, his voice low and lacking its usual authority. 'I hadn't heard you'd chosen badly.'

'This isn't the time to criticize me,' Wyndham said.

Wyndham pointed at the saddle-bag that was identical to the one that had contained the bounty. Granville glanced at the bag and frowned, as if he hadn't been aware that he was holding it.

He held it out and Wyndham moved over to him and took it. While walking back he glanced inside, winced, and then passed it to Matthew.

'What do you want me to say?' Granville asked.

'Talk,' Wyndham said with a gruff voice. 'Tell me something that'll stop me arresting you.'

'You know me and that should be good enough for you.'

'A man was seen slipping out of the Hotel Splendour's back door and then coming here. Now I've found you holding two thousand dollars of stolen money. I need an explanation.'

'I have nothing to say.'

The two men stared at each other and, to help him believe that the impossible may be true, Matthew looked inside the bag at the wads of bills. He removed several while shaking his head, but then he noticed a folded bundle.

He gulped and looked at Granville, who responded with a wince, making Wyndham turn.

'What's wrong?' Wyndham asked.

Matthew withdrew the bundle that had been wrapped up in a brown-stained kerchief. When he held it up, the kerchief fell away and revealed a blood-encrusted knife.

5

'He has to be innocent,' Matthew said when Granville Jennings was locked away in a cell.

'When we found him,' Wyndham said, 'he was holding the stolen bounty and a long-bladed knife of the kind that would have been used to kill your brother. I can't remember another innocent man who looked that guilty.'

'My father respected Newman. He wouldn't kill him.'

Wyndham frowned, but then with a sigh he conceded Matthew's point.

'Perhaps in this case Granville looked too guilty. So for the sake of Snake Ridge we keep an open mind. If this is true, nothing can stop Elijah Moon becoming the next mayor.' He held up the bag. 'I'll take this back to Franklin. Hopefully, he'll keep it safe this time.'

Matthew nodded and then headed to

his desk, but when Wyndham had disappeared from view past the window, he turned to the cells. Granville had pointedly ignored him during his arrest and, when he entered the jailhouse, the contemptuous glance his father cast him before he turned his face away suggested that it wouldn't be easy to make him explain himself.

Matthew stopped before the cell and set his hands on his hips. The silence dragged on for several minutes before he spoke.

'It was always likely that one day we'd stand on the opposite sides of a jail cell's bars,' he said, 'but I didn't expect it'd be this way round.'

'This is no laughing matter,' Granville snapped, his eyes flaring until he saw Matthew's smile and he conceded with a nod that he'd been goaded into talking. 'And neither is the sight of you doing what your brother once did and upholding the law in Snake Ridge.'

'You're right, but if you want to leave that cell, you'll need my help.'

'I'd sooner stay here.'

'So your contempt for me is so great, you'd sooner take the blame for something you didn't do while the person who killed Newman walks free.'

Granville had been scowling, but Matthew's last comment made him sigh and hold his head in his hands.

'I hate you,' he said, his voice small. 'The only time you pleased me is when you left town. When you turned to bank robbery, all I wanted was for people to stop associating you with me. Until you returned that was working.'

'Nobody has connected me to my past yet.'

'Which is as it's supposed to be.' Granville looked up. 'Why did Wyndham employ you?'

'Because he'd heard I'd stood up to the Deno brothers in the Horned Moon.'

'And were you impressive that night?'

Matthew shrugged. 'Not really. The tale must have sounded better than it was.'

Granville sat back against the bars, seemingly in control now that he had him at a disadvantage.

'Which makes me wonder who told Wyndham about the incident and whether that man worked for Elijah.'

Matthew winced. 'Are you saying Elijah plans to discredit you when the truth about my time in jail comes out?'

Granville nodded. 'I'd guess that was his plan.'

'Then it's a pity it failed.' Matthew waited until Granville raised an eyebrow. 'You discredited yourself without my help.'

Granville accepted the insult without a flicker.

'I'll put my trust in the court of law that sentenced you. Then I'll defeat Elijah the proper way while you continue to live a lie.'

Matthew stayed with Granville for another fifteen minutes, but the older man ignored his attempts to get him talking about the incident in the mayor's office and so, when Wyndham returned, he headed back to his desk.

'I didn't tell you to question the prisoner,' Wyndham said.

'I thought I could help a man who's behind bars for the first time,' Matthew said, closing the door to the jailhouse. He took a deep breath. 'Because I'm a former jailbird myself.'

Wyndham's eyes opened wide, at least proving that if he had been employed to embarrass Granville, it had been without his knowledge.

'I'll be facing a heap of trouble soon, so make your excuses your best yet.'

Matthew moved away from the jailhouse and sat on the edge of his desk, giving himself time to think. Feeling that no version of events would let him keep his job, he met Wyndham's eye and offered the truth.

'You were sure to find out soon,' he said, 'but I've spent the last ten years in jail for an attempted bank robbery in Rock Pass. I returned to make amends with my family, but my brother got killed and my father doesn't want to know me. Then you offered me a job and so I accepted it to find Newman's killer. Now it seems Granville needs me, but he won't confide in me.'

Wyndham tipped back his hat and paced back and forth twice.

'And Tarrant Blocker, the man you tried to arrest?'

'He's a former partner in crime.'

'Any other names I should know about?'

'Creighton Kendrick is lurking about; the man who killed Bodie threatened me, and there's one other man.' Matthew paused, enjoying providing the final name. 'Elijah Moon.'

'So that's why you got into a fight in his saloon.' When Matthew didn't reply Wyndham resumed pacing. 'Can you prove he has a past?'

'No.'

'Then your past is of no use to me.' Wyndham stopped to consider him, but Matthew reckoned he'd said everything he could and he kept quiet. 'But your future might be.'

'My past life is behind me. From now on I'll uphold the law.'

'Then we have a job to do.' Wyndham gestured at the door. With a sigh of relief, Matthew moved to walk past him, but Wyndham blocked his path. 'But the moment your past stops you doing your duty, you'll join your father in a cell.'

*　*　*

The window to the waiting room in the mayor's office had been closed. The main door was also locked. So Matthew walked around the building.

Earlier he had joined Wyndham on a patrol around town. Matthew hadn't familiarized himself with the atmosphere of the town yet, but Wyndham reckoned that, since Granville's arrest, tension was in the air and that tonight would be a lively one.

At sundown, they split up leaving Matthew to wonder whether, after finding incriminating evidence in the mayor's office, he might also find something to prove Granville's innocence. But his brief consideration of the building had dampened his enthusiasm.

At the back, he looked over the darkened building, noting several windows and another door. He tried them, but couldn't get in, although it made him wonder why, despite all the options, his father had climbed in through a window.

The only answer Matthew could come up with is that the man who had been seen running away from the hotel hadn't been his father and that this man had wanted to be noticed. He looked up at the window to the room in which they'd found Granville.

Matthew flinched. A man was standing at the window looking down at him, but before Matthew could discern his features, he ducked away.

Wasting no time, Matthew hurried to the back door and put a shoulder to it. On the second shove, the door gave way and he burst in.

Only the faint light coming through the doorway illuminated the otherwise darkened corridor ahead and so, with a hand thrust out, Matthew made his tentative way into the heart of the building.

Luckily, the layout was straightforward. By walking straight ahead, he reached the bottom of the stairs and, as he'd heard only his own footfalls and breathing, knew the intruder would still be upstairs. He took the stairs slowly while peering into the darkness that became deeper with every step.

When he reached the top, he had to feel his way along the wall until he reached the door to the main office, which he pushed open, keeping his back to the wall. Faint light was filtering into this room and so he waited for a silent count of ten. When he heard nothing, he went in low.

A man stepped in front of him, his form only an outline. Hands grabbed his shoulders, halted him, and bundled him away.

Matthew went sprawling backwards into the dark corridor where his uncertainty over what was behind him made him stumble and then land with a jarring thud on his rump. He looked up as the door was slammed shut cutting off the light, but he heard breathing confirming that the intruder was now on his side of the door.

Slowly he moved for his gun while working out exactly where the man was.

'Still your hand!' his unseen assailant demanded. His voice was familiar.

Matthew did as he'd been told, accepting that his assailant had been lurking in the dark for a while and that he could see better than he could.

'So you returned to town, but you still haven't got your hands on the bounty.' Matthew forced a laugh. 'Sadly for you, it's no longer here.'

An aggrieved grunt sounded, pleasingly confirming Matthew's theory.

'In the end everybody will get what they deserve, starting with you.'

The comments had let Matthew work out where the man was standing and he reckoned that if he got an opportunity, he could draw and at least wound him. But the fact that the man hadn't shot him meant he must want to drag something more out of this encounter.

'My father's been blamed for stealing the bounty and for killing my brother. I reckon you know more about those crimes than he does.'

Matthew waited for a denial, but his opponent stayed silent. Gradually, his eyes became accustomed to the dark and he picked out the man's outline standing five feet before him.

Then the man's head jerked to the side and a moment later a door creaked downstairs. A thud sounded, followed by a muttered oath.

'Be quiet,' Tarrant Blocker urged, his voice coming from downstairs.

'I'm sure Matthew came in here,' Creighton Kendrick replied. 'But I can't see a thing.'

Whispered comments were exchanged and then footfalls headed down the corridor downstairs.

'Friends of yours?' the gunman whispered.

'Sure,' Matthew said.

His assailant moved forward and grabbed his arm. In short order he was dragged to his feet and turned round to stand at the top of the stairs.

The shuffling sounds halted at the bottom of the stairs. Then Tarrant and Creighton moved into a lighter patch from where they peered up at them.

'So,' the gunman said, 'most of the old gang are back together again.'

'Who's that?' Creighton said, drawing his gun and beckoning Tarrant to stay back.

He aimed up the stairs. Unfortunately, he was uncertain where they were standing and he picked out a spot that would send the slug winging into the ceiling, but it was close enough to worry Matthew's opponent into edging forward.

Gunmetal caught a stray beam of light as the man aimed at Creighton and so Matthew flicked his arm to the side. His fist caught the man's gun arm and veered the gun away.

Then he sought to grab the gun, but his opponent moved backwards quickly and his hand closed on air.

A firm shove to the chest slammed Matthew into the wall, but when he rebounded he took a long pace forward. He saw movement in the dark and so launched a wild punch at the man's form.

Again the blow whistled by short of its target, and the action unbalanced him forcing him to thrust out a leg. His foot landed on air and he realized with a lurch that he'd moved to the top of the stairs.

As he found his footing with a disconcerting lunge on to a lower step, his flailing hand grabbed the banister where he clung on while looking down at the corridor below.

Creighton was coming up the stairs,

but he had adopted the tentative motion that Matthew had used when he'd climbed up. Worse, Creighton had aimed his gun at him.

'It's me,' Matthew said. 'Don't — '

He didn't get to complete his demand as his assailant pushed him from behind and sent him sprawling over the banister. He suffered a dizzying view of the floor below. Then his unbalanced weight made his feet leave the stairs and his body slid over the rail.

In desperation, he tightened his grip around the banister and, when he came to rest, he was dangling one-handed. The strain on his arm in an awkward position threatened to tear him away, but with a frantic gesture, his free hand caught a stair rail and steadied him.

'Where did he go?' Creighton said, now at his side.

Matthew glanced up and saw the office door swing open.

'That way,' he said.

Creighton leaned over the rail to consider his predicament.

'You rest up,' he said. 'I'll deal with him.'

Then he hurried off. When Tarrant arrived a few moments later, he asked the other obvious question.

'Who is he?'

'Quit asking questions,' Matthew said through clenched teeth, 'and help me.'

Tarrant nodded and then gathered a firm grip around his chest. After several failed attempts, he resorted to tugging on his jacket and, in an ungainly sprawl, he dragged him back over the rail.

'You've been helped,' he said when both men were standing against the wall. 'So answer the question.'

'I've got no idea who he is, but he knows us and, from what just happened, I'd guess he bears us a grudge.'

A gunshot sounded, but the noise was muffled, as if it were distant and not from inside the building. The two men glanced at each other and nodded. Then they hurried up the stairs.

At the door, Tarrant drew his gun, but waved Matthew on. As he hurried through the door, Matthew smiled, finding that he enjoyed working again with an old friend. With his head down, he headed for the desk where he hunkered down to cover Tarrant as he came in.

Tarrant had yet to reach him when he confirmed that the office was deserted. Then he saw the open door to the other office, which was bathed in light.

He set off, with Tarrant at his heels, and before he reached the door he saw Creighton at the window, looking down as the intruder had done earlier, except this time the window was open.

'Gone,' Creighton said when he heard them coming into the room. 'He was too quick for me.'

Matthew joined him at the window where he again heard gunfire, this time clearly from outside.

'Sounds like he's facing some trouble out there.'

'I don't think so. That's coming from some distance away.'

Matthew nodded, but then with a

wince he remembered how his life had changed today, something he'd forgotten about during the chaos of the last few minutes.

'I have to go,' he said, turning away.

'You wanted to be a lawman,' Tarrant called after him, making him stop at the door.

'I did and I'm obliged you two helped me, but as I can't talk about you or what happened here, from now on stay out of my way.'

'I understand.' Tarrant waited until Matthew started to go through the door. 'But working together again felt good, didn't it?'

Matthew's only response was to halt for a moment before he hurried away.

6

When Matthew joined Marshal Wyndham outside the Lucky Star Saloon, people were spilling out on to the boardwalk, fleeing from the sporadic gunfire that was ringing out inside.

'It seems,' Wyndham said, 'that Elijah's set out to make things worse for Granville by discrediting Franklin.'

'Why are you sure this is his doing?' Matthew asked. He looked for a way into the saloon, but too many people filled the doorway for him to make headway.

'Because Franklin owns the saloon and there's never been trouble in here before.'

Matthew nodded and then moved people aside as he sought a route forward. Wyndham tried a different path along the wall and found a gap that let him reach the door ten feet ahead of Matthew.

When he slipped through the doorway and moved out of view, Matthew re-doubled his efforts, anger at the unresolved mysteries of the last few hours spurring him on.

Without consideration, he barged people aside until he reached the doorway. The last stragglers were escaping and so he burst through the press of people into clear space to see that a stand-off was in progress.

One man lay on his chest in the middle of the saloon room, unmoving. Three men had taken refuge behind a tangle of upturned tables in a corner of the saloon where they'd turned their guns on another two men who were hiding behind the bar.

'Stay out of this, lawman,' one of those men was saying as Matthew joined Wyndham.

'You don't give the orders,' Wyndham said. 'Put down your guns.'

'We can't.' The two men stood up from behind the bar and pointed at the dead man, letting Matthew see that they were the Deno brothers. 'They started this when they attacked Wilson.'

'Wilson Coney?' Wyndham and Matthew both said.

Matthew had met Granville's mild-mannered official only once before. Although he had been irritating, he was the last man he'd expect to start a gunfight in a saloon.

Before he could share that view with Wyndham, the men in the corner raised their six-shooters and fired at the bar, making Abraham and Lawrence dive for cover.

With the brothers then staying down, Matthew glanced at Wyndham for his reaction. But the problem of who they should side with when everybody appeared to be in the wrong was decided for them when one of the men in the corner took a shot at them.

The slug clattered into the wall several feet above their heads, but neither man took a chance and together they scurried for safety behind the nearest table. Wyndham reached it first. He hunkered down and rested his gun on the table where he picked out the shooter.

By the time Matthew scrambled into cover beside him, Wyndham was firing. On his second shot, a cry of pain sounded and the gunman stood up from behind the table with a red bloom spreading across his chest.

He fell forward to lie over the table with his arms dangling. He twitched once and then stilled. Then his weight made the table topple over to reveal the other two gunmen, who made a rapid decision to run for the bar while firing at the brothers.

Their desperate action encouraged the brothers to jump up and, as slugs tore into the bar and the wall behind the brothers, Wyndham and Matthew joined them in blasting lead at the running men.

Rapid gunfire ripped out and within moments the two gunmen stomped to a faltering halt, their forms peppered with so many bullets Matthew wasn't sure which of their wounds he'd inflicted. Then they sank to their knees.

One man had received a slug to the neck that felled him like a tree. He didn't move again.

The final man clutched his stomach before trying to raise his gun to aim at the bar, but a second shot from Abraham slammed into his forehead. He rocked backwards and stared at the ceiling with dead eyes. Then, silently he fell to the side.

'Enough!' Wyndham demanded.

'They heard you, lawman,' Elijah Moon said as he slipped in through the doorway to consider the scene. 'Unlike those men, my men are law-abiding.'

The statement had been directed at the customers who were cowering in the corners of the saloon room and those who were close by outside, but Matthew didn't mind as it clarified why this fight had really erupted. He got up from behind the table to consider the mayhem.

Following their boss's order, the smirking Deno brothers came round the bar and stood before the bodies with their guns aimed upwards.

While Wyndham covered him, Matthew checked on the shot men. They were all dead. He recognized only Wilson Coney; he had been peppered with at least four gunshot wounds.

'In the year I've been Snake Ridge's marshal,' Wyndham said, also speaking loudly for everyone's benefit, 'there's never been so much as a serious wounding in the Lucky Star. Now, on the day I find the stolen bounty in the mayor's office and as a precaution I have to arrest the mayor's assistant, four men are killed, one being the mayor's trusted official.'

Elijah chuckled. 'You can't trust some people. Perhaps my tough approach will be better for Snake Ridge than the slimy ways of Franklin Buxton's paid thief, Granville Jennings.'

'I'm sure this mess was supposed to make everyone think that, but I know

Franklin. He'll never give in to intimidation, and Granville will still stand for mayor.'

Elijah snarled, but Wyndham pre-empted any threats he might provide by gesturing at Matthew to claim the brothers' guns.

'Hey,' Elijah said as Matthew held out a hand, 'they were only defending themselves.'

'I don't know what went on in here yet,' Wyndham said, 'but from what I can see, these two men are guiltier than Granville Jennings is. I only found incriminating evidence in the mayor's office whereas they're packing guns, something everyone knows I don't allow.'

The gunmen glanced at Elijah and, when he nodded, they handed over their weapons.

'I won't accept this quietly,' Elijah said.

'I'm sure you won't, but if you utter one more word of complaint, I'll put you in the cell next to theirs.' He glanced at Matthew. 'Take them away.'

When Matthew led the brothers to the door, the customers who were edging back into the saloon nodded with approval. At the door, Elijah leaned towards him.

'Tonight started Snake Ridge's troubles,' he whispered. 'Noon tomorrow will end yours.'

★   ★   ★

All five cells in the jailhouse were full, but at least the night of mayhem appeared to be over.

Wyndham and Matthew slumped down on their chairs behind their desks and clutched steaming mugs of coffee to their chests. Neither man was in the mood to talk about the earlier incidents that clearly had been orchestrated, but which had nevertheless achieved their objectives.

So the room was silent other than the ticking clock and the prisoners' grumbling.

Earlier that evening, after the gunfight in the Lucky Star, there'd been a second assault on Franklin's business interests, this time at the Hotel Cactus Flower, his smaller hotel. The storeman from the mercantile opposite the Hotel Moonshine had picked a fight with another man in the lobby.

Nobody knew what the argument had been about, but their squabble had dragged other people into the fray. When the lawmen arrived, furniture and windows had been broken, and the noise had driven worried guests out into the road.

The target had been beaten badly and he'd needed treatment from Doc Hamilton, but he hadn't wanted to talk about the incident. Despite this, a reprisal attack on the mercantile from a group of club-wielding men had followed, leaving the mercantile stock destroyed and the store trashed.

The storeman hadn't wanted to talk about that incident either.

Before Matthew and Wyndham could

work out the chain of events leading to the attacks, the fights had generated their own wave of madness.

Someone had started a fire in a room in the Hotel Splendour. Then there'd been another shooting over a spilt drink, although it hadn't been fatal.

As the night wore on, people who were usually peaceful had picked fights with others, and then the losers had gone on to pick other fights.

The early trouble had taken place in Franklin's establishments and someone connected to Elijah had always been involved. But many of the later incidents had nothing to do with them, and that worried the lawmen the most.

It meant one man really could encourage a peaceful town to destroy itself with a few well-judged actions.

'You reckon we're over the worst of it?' Matthew asked, breaking the thoughtful silence.

'I can only hope,' Wyndham said with a weary sigh. 'Come the morning the decent folk will be ashamed of what they did tonight, but the tension will simmer on and another spark could relight the fuse.'

'And to think that all that trouble started because Wilson Coney got roaring drunk and made threats in the Lucky Star.'

Wyndham snorted a rueful laugh and put down his coffee mug. He stood and paced to the window to look at the dark road.

'Obliged you reminded me about that. Unpicking all the threads of tonight's trouble might be impossible, but that's one event we can poke at until the truth comes out.'

'I assume Wilson didn't trouble you much before tonight?'

'I only saw him when he did his duty.' Wyndham turned from the window. 'And that was to keep me from seeing the mayor.'

'So what do you reckon happened?'

'Wilson hadn't been seen since we found the bounty in the mayor's office. Then he arrived in the Lucky Star and was so drunk he couldn't stand up and had to be helped along by Abraham and Lawrence. Unfortunately, he walked in the direction of three surly newcomers to town.'

Matthew nodded, fitting in the rest of the story for himself. The brothers had forced liquor down Wilson's throat until he was half-comatose, and then they'd provoked an argument that had resulted in him being shot up.

'The jailhouse is full, so I can fit Elijah into a cell — that's if you've got enough to bring him in.'

'I haven't. And with all this chaos, we're no nearer to connecting him to your brother's murder.' Wyndham paced across the office and considered him, as if expecting him to volunteer information. 'Unless you know what he meant when he warned you about noon tomorrow.'

Matthew winced, having thought that nobody else had heard that exchange.

'Earlier today, he gave me an ultimatum to leave town. It expires at noon tomorrow.'

Wyndham nodded. 'Are you leaving?'

'Nope.'

'Good. If every threatened lawman ran away, there'd be no lawmen left.' Wyndham slapped his shoulder. 'But at least that means he's worried.'

'Why?'

'Because when men use words instead of bullets, they're trying to scare you off. The serious threats come with bullets instead of words.'

Matthew nodded. He stood up and headed to the window.

Despite the low light level outside, he saw a man smoking across the road. Then the glow of light dropped to the ground and fizzled out as the man stepped back into the shadows.

'Whether the threat's serious or not,' Matthew said, 'I reckon I'll stay here until that noon deadline.'

7

The morning sun brought with it a reckoning, and it was the one Wyndham had predicted.

When Matthew distributed the morning meal, most of the prisoners looked cowed. Shame had replaced the anger that had driven them on the night before. Out of the twenty prisoners crowding the cells, only the ringleaders were still surly.

Matthew stopped at the final cell to consider the most morose prisoner, his father. A night in a cell appeared to have done the one thing Matthew would never have expected and broken his spirit.

Granville sat on the floor with his back to the bars and his legs drawn up to his chest, staring at a fixed point before him. He didn't react when Matthew passed in food and neither did the prisoners give him his share.

Matthew tried to catch his eye, but failed and so, feeling as forlorn as his father looked, he headed back to the main office where Wyndham was returning from his morning patrol.

'Quiet?' Matthew asked.

'People are clearing up and Franklin is still defiant, so I hope everyone will avoid getting dragged into whatever Elijah tries next.' Wyndham considered the jailhouse door. 'So this is the time to make a point. Release everyone we dragged in last night who's not connected to Elijah Moon.'

Matthew didn't mention that even if Franklin was defiant, his father appeared to have given up.

Wyndham sat at his desk and, when Matthew opened the cells, he gave every passing man a stern glare. Nobody met his eye, although a few mumbled apologies.

When Matthew had reduced the prisoners to just five of Elijah's men and his father, the lawmen drank coffee and waited, but the morning drifted by without incident.

When it became clear that Elijah wouldn't retaliate immediately, Matthew considered his last encounter with his mysterious opponent. Unfortunately, he couldn't concentrate on the event as his thoughts kept returning to his deadline and, even though he tried not to, his gaze never strayed far from the clock on the wall.

'I'll check,' he said when thirty minutes remained, 'that it's still quiet out there.'

'At least that'll stop you watching the clock,' Wyndham said, joining him. 'Come on. Let's see what Elijah does.'

'Obliged,' Matthew said with a grateful smile.

Outside, the two men leaned back against the law office wall. It was quiet other than the people going about their business, all of whom made a point of coming over and chatting. Elijah didn't appear.

For as long as he could, Matthew

resisted the urge to check on the time and so, when he looked through the window, it was ten minutes past the hour.

'Are you sure he meant noon today?' Wyndham said with a smile.

Matthew returned the smile. 'He did, but as you said, Elijah's threat was just words.'

'Against you it was.' Wyndham turned away. 'But now that we've dealt with your problem, I'll see about the rest of the town. Stay here and look after our guests.'

With that, Wyndham headed away leaving Matthew to take a last look along the road before he went inside. He had taken only a few paces when he heard a raised voice coming from the jailhouse.

'What's wrong?' Matthew called as he made his slow way across the office.

'One of your prisoners is ill,' Abraham called back making Matthew stop and look aloft, sighing.

He resolved that from now on he'd

let himself enjoy his new role because, for the first time, he could see how his past would help him. He'd been a prisoner and so he knew the ruses they used to create diversions.

This ruse was one of the most obvious.

Planning to use the situation to make a point, he walked to the door slowly and let himself in, but the moment he closed the door his good mood died. His father was the one in trouble.

He was lying curled up on the floor and, as he was the only prisoner in his cell, when Matthew burst in, he left his cell door open. He knelt at his side, put a hand on his shoulder, and then rolled him over.

Granville slumped on to his back to reveal a face that was mottled with red marks, although Matthew was relieved to see he was breathing.

'How long has he been like this?' Matthew said, rocking back to give him air.

'Since noon,' Abraham said from behind him.

The statement's intent had just registered when a hand clamped around his chin and jerked him backwards. Too late Matthew noted that the Deno brothers were in the cell next to his father's and that the red marks on his face were bruises and not the sign of an illness.

He was dragged to his feet. Then an arm was wrapped around his throat while he was held against the bars. In short order Abraham disarmed him and then removed his ring of keys.

'You did this?' Matthew said as Lawrence put a key to his cell door.

'The same trick worked on the father and then on the son,' Abraham gloated in his ear. 'You'd think a jailbird would know better than to fall for this old ruse.'

'Be quiet. You're making this worse for yourself, and for Elijah,' said Matthew.

The mention of Elijah made Abraham tighten his grip, cutting off Matthew's windpipe and forcing him to struggle. He put both hands to

Abraham's arms and tugged, but his assailant had a firm grip around his neck and easily held him in place.

Motes of light flickered at the corners of his vision and then more worryingly patches of darkness grew.

'Leave him,' Lawrence said, his voice seemingly coming from a distance.

After straining to tighten his grip even more, Abraham snorted a laugh and then released him. Matthew dropped to the floor to lie beside his father where he gasped in air.

He put his hands to the floor to lever himself up, but the effort failed and so he curled up and conserved his strength while awaiting their next move. That turned out to be locking his door and then opening the other cells.

With much whooping, the freed prisoners trooped out into the law office, although Abraham stayed to look at him through the bars.

'Your father's beating was your only warning,' he said with a smirk. 'The applications for mayor have to be in by noon tomorrow. Leave town by then — if you still have a job to leave.'

Then he hurried after Lawrence leaving Matthew alone in the cell with his father.

★　★　★

'Will he be all right?' Wyndham asked when Matthew came out of the doctor's surgery.

'He's conscious but he's resting,' Matthew said. 'He got knocked out and he's covered in bruises, so he must have been beaten for all the time we were outside. For a man used to respect, that's tough to accept.'

Matthew didn't add that he was putting words into his father's mouth as, even though Granville had come to in the surgery, he'd refused to talk to him. But, from the stern look that Wyndham then gave him, he would have welcomed his boss also punishing him with silence.

'And now,' Wyndham said, drawing

him back to the wall where they'd be out of sight on the busy road, 'you'll explain yourself.'

Matthew frowned. 'My father was in trouble. I let down my guard.'

'You've been my deputy for one day. In that time the man I sent you to escort into town got shot up, you disobeyed my order, you annoyed Franklin Buxton, I find out you're a jailbird, and now you've been locked in your own cell. What mistakes will you surprise me with next?'

Matthew opened his mouth planning to mention the things he had done right, but then wisely he chose the alternate line.

'I'll bring the prisoners back, starting with the Deno brothers.'

Wyndham treated him to a short nod of approval.

'The rest follow their lead, so I'll settle for those two. And find them quickly before word gets out and we become a laughing stock.'

Matthew turned away smartly while

he still had a job and set about completing his mission. Firstly, he visited the Horned Moon, which, in the early afternoon, was quiet.

The bartender who had served him two days ago was on duty. He appraised his new status and provided evasive answers, but Matthew judged that his studied disdain meant the brothers hadn't returned there.

He tried two other saloons before he ended up standing outside the Full Moon Hotel where Elijah lived. He stared up at the windows in the hope that Elijah would come down and they could confront each other in full view.

When he didn't appear, he headed inside.

'Go away,' the surly desk clerk said before he could even state his business.

Then, presumably in response to an unseen signal, four men emerged from the shadows and loitered around the bottom of the stairs. Matthew still headed for the stairs until the men closed ranks, forcing him to stop.

'Get out of my way,' Matthew said. 'I'm looking for escaped prisoners.'

'Don't see no prisoners here,' the nearest man said with a mocking smile. 'All I see is a deputy who got locked in his own cell.'

The other three men laughed and then peered at him with eager grins as they awaited his response.

'That cell's now empty, but it won't be for long if you men don't stand aside.'

The men glanced at each other seeing who wanted to be the next one to pour scorn on him, but before anyone could speak Elijah appeared at the top of the stairs. Walking slowly, he came down.

'I'm surprised you're still here,' he said. He stopped on the middle stair. 'I thought your father's beating should have been warning enough that you should get out of town.'

'And was my brother's death a warning to my father?'

Elijah curled his lip in a sneer. 'Take

your unfounded accusations elsewhere.'

'The only place I'm going is upstairs to look for the Deno brothers.'

'They're not here. Neither are you.'

Elijah raised a hand and, with a crisp movement, the four men advanced on him. Matthew batted away the first man to put a hand on him, but that only encouraged the others to co-ordinate their assault.

Hands slammed down on his shoulders while a second man grabbed his waist and a third gripped his arms. Matthew planted his feet wide apart and struggled, but there were too many of them and he couldn't dislodge even one man. Seeing no alternative, he stopped squirming.

'You sure do act tough, Elijah,' he shouted as he was manhandled to the door, 'when all these men separate me from you.'

'Take that as proof that you'll never touch me,' Elijah said, unconcerned at the taunt. 'But annoy me again and I'll do what I did to you ten years ago in Rock Pass.'

Elijah considered him as he was dragged backwards, his smirk defying him to work out what he had meant.

'Ten years ago a heap of lawmen descended on me in Rock Pass when I — ' Matthew dug in his heels and halted his progress as the terrible truth hit him. 'They were waiting for me because you warned them I was coming! Then, when I got arrested, you double-crossed Creighton and Tarrant and stole the money.'

Elijah laughed. 'I'm pleased you've figured it out in the end.'

'So did you frame my father?' He waited for an answer, but Elijah didn't reply other than to continue smiling as he enjoyed his distress. 'Are you using that man who's lurking around in the shadows near the mayor's office?'

Elijah tensed, his good mood ending in a moment and, with an angry muttered oath, he swung round and headed back up the stairs.

Elijah's revelations made Matthew try to buck his captors, but they held him firmly. Then they walked him through the door and, for his troubles, one man delivered a firm kick to the rump that knocked him to the ground outside.

He got up slowly and took his time in batting the dust from his knees. Then, with his neck burning from the feeling that he was being watched from the upstairs windows, he headed back to the prosperous part of town.

He didn't look back and cheered himself with the thought that if the escaped prisoners had decided to hole up in the Full Moon Hotel, the day might not be as rowdy as he'd feared. Like yesterday afternoon, the town was quiet and, like yesterday, the first signs of animated activity came when he reached the Hotel Splendour.

Again, when he looked through the window, the staff was milling around while Franklin berated them. He went in.

'What's happened this time?' he called.

Silence descended as Franklin turned to him. Worry creased his face.

'We need help,' he said. 'I was hoping I was wrong, but I'm not. My son Jimmy's gone missing.'

With so many other problems to worry about, Matthew had put his concerns about Franklin's son from his mind. But when Abigail came out from behind the reception desk and shot him a narrow-eyed look that warned him not to mention his theory, he had to grip his hands into tight fists to concentrate.

'Jimmy?' he murmured, lost for an appropriate reply.

'Yes,' Franklin said. 'He left to take a pile of sheets upstairs, but he never returned. He's not been seen for half an hour.'

Matthew turned on the spot, presenting the air of a man who was sizing up the scene, while in reality he had to force his mind to stop racing so that he could consider the rapidly worsening situation.

An hour had passed since his mistake had let the prisoners escape and that meant the Deno brothers were the most likely culprits. He didn't think this information would help and so he offered a comforting smile.

'Boys are always sneaking away, but he won't have gone far. Keep looking and let me know when he returns.'

Franklin searched his eyes and then shook his head.

'Don't mince words with me. I know you reckon Elijah's kidnapped him to browbeat me into withdrawing my support for Granville.' Franklin lowered his voice. 'So when you see Elijah, tell him it's worked. I resisted everything he tried last night, but nothing is more important to me than my son's life.'

'If it's any consolation,' Matthew said with a gulp, 'if Jimmy were my son, I'd do the same.'

Luckily, Franklin was looking at Abigail and so he didn't see that

Matthew's unwise comment set off a tremor in his neck. He had to rub the back of his neck to stop himself shaking, and Abigail must have seen his discomfort as she took Franklin's arm and led him away.

'I'm obliged for your support,' Franklin called over his shoulder. At the door behind the desk he stopped and stared straight ahead with his shoulders hunched. 'But don't tell Elijah that the moment he's released Jimmy, I'll kill him.'

Matthew didn't risk repeating his previous sentiment. When Franklin and Abigail went through the door, he checked that the dispersing staff weren't watching him. Then he headed upstairs to room seven.

He knocked and, after a few scuffing noises had sounded within, Tarrant Blocker bade him to enter. He went in and nodded to Tarrant, who, as before, was sitting at the window.

Then he looked behind the door and

smiled at the lurking Creighton Kendrick.

'What do you want with us now?' Creighton asked.

Matthew headed across the room to the window. He looked at the mayor's office where last night these men's intervention had probably saved his life. Then he looked further afield to the heavily guarded Full Moon Hotel, the most likely place the boy had been taken.

'I reckon,' he said, 'it's time for us to join forces.'

8

'How are we going to get in there?' Tarrant said, peering at the Full Moon Hotel from around the corner of the Horned Moon Saloon.

'You once claimed that your light fingers could get you into any building, room or safe,' Matthew said, and when Creighton snorted a laugh, he turned to him. 'And you once claimed that you could work out a plan to — '

'That was only,' Creighton said with a smile, 'after you'd given me the details of the layout and the people we'd face. Which you haven't.'

This time Matthew laughed and, with their spirits raised, they exchanged ideas on how they'd sneak into Elijah's domain. None of their ideas sounded foolproof as the building stood isolated from the buildings around it and its many windows meant it couldn't be approached without them being noticed.

So for the next hour they waited, hoping that something unexpected would happen and provide them with a distraction, but few people came close to the hotel.

Creighton was starting to outline his best idea — a complex plan involving disguises, a covered wagon, and a fire — when they had the luck they'd been hoping for.

A rider drew up outside the hotel and hurried inside. A few minutes later, Elijah came out accompanied by the men who had assaulted Matthew earlier. Elijah's expression was thunderous and, without discussion, the men went to their horses and then rode off at a gallop behind the rider.

Matthew and his group ducked into the saloon to avoid being seen, but the men didn't look their way and carried on towards the railroad tracks beyond the edge of town.

'That looked like he got bad news,' Tarrant said.

'It did,' Matthew said, 'but the more important thing is, aside from the desk clerk, those were the only men I saw in the hotel.'

'So,' Creighton said, 'Jimmy's kidnappers could be the only ones we'll have to take on.'

This optimistic outlook made everyone smile and so, at a calm pace, they headed out of the saloon. On the way to the hotel, Matthew watched the windows, but didn't see anyone looking out. When they reached the door, he beckoned the others to stop.

'Before we go any further,' he said, 'we need to agree on what we're looking for here.'

'We want the money that's rightfully ours,' Creighton said. 'But kidnapping that kid was wrong. So we free the kid first and we get our money back second.'

Matthew glanced at Tarrant who provided a sharp nod.

'Obliged,' Matthew said. He turned to the door, but Creighton slapped a hand on his arm and drew him back.

'But if the kid's not there, we still want our money.'

Creighton gripped his arm tightly, effectively asking the question that had been on Matthew's mind since he'd decided to join them.

'I won't help you steal,' he declared, 'but I won't stop you either.'

'That's good enough for us,' Creighton said. He raised his hand and, with that, the three men slipped inside quietly.

Unlike the last time, the surly desk clerk wasn't on duty, although Matthew heard people moving around nearby. The three men huddled and exchanged nods and gestures debating their next move.

Then they peered into the rooms downstairs, none of which were occupied other than the room behind the reception desk in which six men were milling around. There was no sign of Jimmy and so, in single file, they headed for the stairs. They reached the upstairs floor without being confronted.

Matthew tried the first door on the corridor, finding it unlocked, but it presented only a basic room with a bed and a chair, as did the next two doors. But the final door on the corridor had a more solid construction and it was locked.

Tarrant was at the back and, with a chuckle, he put hands to both men's arms and pushed them aside. Then he slipped between them, while grinning and waggling his fingers as he got his first opportunity to demonstrate his talent.

Within a minute the door swung open to reveal opulent leather chairs, numerous engraved cupboards, and a desk that was the same design as the one in the mayor's office, except this one was larger.

Tarrant stayed at the door while Creighton tried the only other door in the room, which led into a small, unoccupied bedroom.

'This has to be Elijah's lair,' Tarrant

whispered, 'but there's no sign of that kid being held hostage up here.'

Matthew nodded. Then, while Creighton searched the room, he and Tarrant tried the rest of the doors. All but one of them opened to reveal a basic bedroom that didn't appear to have been occupied recently.

The last room didn't have a bed, but it had several chairs, along with a table on which a poker game had been left abandoned. The stench of tobacco, whiskey and sweat suggested that the men who had confronted him earlier had used this room until they'd left with Elijah.

When he and Tarrant returned to Elijah's office, Creighton was sitting at the desk leafing through a ledger.

'He's used our money to good effect,' he said. 'He could return it to us ten times over and still stay in business.'

As he'd failed in his main objective, Matthew bade Creighton to guard the door while he took over trying to unravel the details of Elijah's business dealings. He wasn't sure what to look for, but hoped he might come across something that would link him to Newman.

While he rummaged, Tarrant wandered around the room looking for valuables. Matthew judged that a haul of the more valuable trinkets that he picked up, appraised, and then put down in the same place might satisfy his colleagues. But Tarrant continued looking for something more valuable and, after fifteen minutes, he found it.

He got both men's attention with an excited wave and then, with a flourish, he opened the innocuous looking cupboard in the corner.

Both men came over to look at the empty interior, but before they could scoff about his mistake, Tarrant removed a hook that was hanging on the back of the door. With a knowing wink, he used it to lever away the false back of the cupboard.

He propped the wood against the wall and then stood aside to let

Creighton and Matthew see that set into the wall was a safe. With another waggle of the fingers, Tarrant got to work.

As this meant they would be leaving soon, Matthew returned to the desk and set about putting the ledger and other items he'd been reading back where he'd found them.

'Anything incriminating?' Tarrant asked as he worked.

Matthew shook his head. 'As far as I could make out, he's recorded only his legitimate, and lucrative, business transactions.'

'A man who keeps good records probably also details the less legitimate transactions.'

Matthew cast a glance at Tarrant that said that although he agreed, time was pressing. Then, bearing in mind how Tarrant had found the safe, he patted the bottom of each drawer. They all returned solid sounds and so he peered inside and checked the depth of the drawers against the width of the desk.

The bottom drawer turned out to be less deep than the others and so, using a key, he pried open the back of the drawer to reveal a thin journal. He flicked through it noting the neat rows of names and numbers.

'Got something?' Creighton asked.

'I don't know what it is.' Matthew slipped the book in his pocket. 'But Elijah wanted it kept secret, so it must be important.'

'But not,' Tarrant called from the corner, 'as important as this.'

When he had both men's attention, he swung open the safe door to reveal three shelves of packed contents, but just as Tarrant started smiling, a heavy thud sounded.

'That was too loud,' Creighton said.

'I know, but it's been a while since . . . ' Tarrant trailed off and then looked aloft, shaking his head. He swirled round to face Creighton. 'Sorry. I didn't notice the tripwire. I reckon I set off an alarm.'

A moment later he was proved

correct when raised voices sounded downstairs.

'Grab what you can,' Creighton urged, slipping out into the corridor. 'Then run.'

Tarrant located a folded bag in the bottom of the safe and quickly he shoved handfuls of bills and several boxes that rattled into the bag before slamming the safe door shut. Then he joined Matthew in hurrying to the door.

As an afterthought, Matthew doubled back to the desk and swept the ledgers to the floor to add to the confusion. When he joined the other two men in the corridor, he heard footfalls pounding up the stairs.

He judged that more than one man was coming for them. So, with only seconds to act, he left the door open and they slipped into the room two doors down, the furthest room they could reach.

Creighton had just closed the door when the men reached the corridor. He and Creighton stayed by the door while Tarrant headed to the window.

As they hoped, the men ran by their room and hurried into Elijah's office. Cries of alarm sounded. Then they dashed out into the corridor and threw open the first door.

Tarrant co-ordinated their pursuers' actions with the moment he pushed open the window and, when he glanced down and nodded, the other two men hurried over to join him.

With discovery imminent, Tarrant had no choice but to hurl the bag through the window. Then he swung his legs over the sill and lowered himself down. He hung on to the sill for a moment before dropping.

Creighton and then Matthew followed his lead with neither man delaying to check on how close their pursuers were. Just as Matthew sat on the sill, the door swung open.

He quickly dropped down to dangle before releasing his grip. He landed on the soft earth at the back of the hotel with knees bent.

He still stumbled backwards, but Creighton grabbed him and stilled his progress. Then the three men ran for the corner of the building, reaching it before the men upstairs looked through the window.

'Scatter,' Matthew said, receiving nods from Tarrant and Creighton and, with no time to even debate where they'd meet up, they ran off in different directions.

While clutching the bag to his chest, Tarrant picked a route that took him away from the front door and into the heart of town. Matthew ran across the road, while Creighton ran towards the door aiming to go past it and run to the outskirts of town.

When Matthew reached the other side of the road, he glanced over his shoulder. To his relief, Tarrant was no longer visible while Creighton's distraction had worked. He'd been seen and so four of the men who had come out of the hotel were chasing him while only two men were heading across the road after him.

Nobody appeared to be following Tarrant.

Matthew turned on his heel and ran. Within a minute, he reached the corner of the road.

Then he pounded down the board-walk aiming to head to the law office. He had covered only a few dozen yards when he saw Marshal Wyndham walking towards him.

'Trouble?' Wyndham called.

'It's nothing I can't handle,' Matthew shouted.

He slowed to a halt and glanced over his shoulder as his pursuers rounded the corner. These men took one look at the approaching lawman and doubled-back.

'Like all of Elijah's men they haven't got much fight in them,' Wyndham said when he joined him. 'But I don't like seeing my deputy running away. What did you catch them doing?'

'I was looking for Franklin's son. I

reckon Elijah kidnapped him.'

'So do I. I'm going to the Full Moon Hotel to question him.'

'You won't find him there. He left town twenty minutes ago.' Matthew pointed, signalling the railroad tracks that headed east towards Hunter's Pass. Then he considered Wyndham's stern gaze and, although he was sure that his boss wouldn't appreciate the explanation, he pressed on anyhow. 'So, with Elijah gone, I went to his hotel.'

'And those men wouldn't let you in?'

'I sneaked in. They chased me out.'

For long moments Wyndham considered him. Then he took a step backwards while looking around to check that nobody was close.

'This time I'll accept the blame for your mistake. You stood up to Elijah Moon's men and I thought that made you a good man to deputize. But now I can see that a jailbird thinks like a man who evades the law and not like a lawman who upholds it.'

'I tried to find a kidnapped child,'

Matthew snapped. 'You're not telling me I was wrong to do that.'

'You weren't wrong, but the way you did it was. If you reckoned Elijah kidnapped Jimmy, you should have followed him out of town.'

'I thought Jimmy was being held in the hotel.'

'Then you should have gone through the front door and demanded to be shown every room. If someone stood in your way, you should have arrested him, not run away.'

Matthew lowered his head, struggling for a suitable answer. Wyndham was right, but he couldn't tell him what he'd really been doing.

'Either way, Jimmy wasn't there and I don't reckon he ever was.'

'Then the bad news keeps mounting up for that family. Franklin headed out to Snake Gorge, presumably to search for his boy. I followed his tracks and found him lying beneath the bridge, all broke up and unconscious.'

Matthew winced. 'Fell off the bridge or pushed off?'

'I don't know.' Wyndham pointed at the surgery. 'So while I do what you should have done and find out why Elijah headed out of town, sit with Franklin in case he wakes up and talks.'

'Sure.'

Matthew moved on, but after a few paces, Wyndham called him back.

'And take this is as your last warning, Deputy Jennings,' he said. 'Start acting like a lawman, or I'll be giving you a new noon deadline to leave town.'

9

'I've been told to stay here until Franklin comes to,' Matthew said, opting for a different method after his first dozen attempts to get his father to acknowledge him had failed. 'So it might be easier to talk than to stay quiet.'

A tightening of the skin around his eyes was Granville's only reaction, but it was enough for Matthew. He'd often been incarcerated with men he hated, and experience told him that persistence always defeated the attempt to punish someone with silence.

'I have some good news,' Matthew said in an encouraging tone. 'Marshal Wyndham says that if you promise to stay here, you don't have to return to a cell. You're still under arrest, though.'

Granville said nothing and so Matthew settled down on the chair beside his father's bed and waited for Doc Hamilton to emerge. He'd been treating Franklin when Matthew had arrived and after thirty minutes, he was still working on him. Abigail was with them.

With nothing else to occupy his mind, he looked Granville over, noting that he appeared comfortable although when he moved so that he could avoid looking at him, he did so stiffly.

'Do you want any help?' Matthew asked, moving forward.

Granville eyed the unoccupied bed beside him, but then settled for lying on his side facing away from his son.

'I can remember me doing the same to you when I was ten years old,' Matthew persisted. 'I was sick and you wanted me to drink this foul-smelling, putrid concoction. I ignored you, but every time I turned my head away, you followed me. I drank it in the end. Then I threw up. Then I got better.' Matthew laughed. 'I still feel sick whenever I see a stinging nettle, though.'

Granville hunched his shoulders

higher, but then, as if the accusation that he was acting childishly had hit a nerve, he sat upright on his bed looking forward.

He still didn't look at him or speak, and Matthew decided to be silent for a while and grant him the dignity of not having to ignore everything he said.

Presently Doc Hamilton came out of the surgery with Abigail in tow. She took one look at him and then turned on her heel to go back into the surgery, leaving Hamilton to face Matthew.

'It's too early to say if he'll live,' Hamilton said. 'I've splinted his broken bones, but he had a bad knock on the head and that leaves his fate in the hands of a higher power than mine.'

'I assume he said nothing about who did it?' Matthew watched Hamilton shake his head, so he continued. 'Or about what he was doing out at the bridge? Or whether he'd found a clue about where Jimmy had been taken?'

'He wasn't conscious enough to say anything intelligible and I can't answer your questions either. All I know is Wyndham found him lying at the bottom of the bridge and he's been lucky to survive for this long.'

Abigail had left the door open and the final comment made her return, her face red and her eyes puffy. She gestured at Matthew.

'If you'd done your job properly and found Jimmy,' she said, her voice croaking, 'he wouldn't have been out there. He . . . '

An uncontrollable sob made her trail off. Matthew didn't reply, finding that this time he didn't mind being the butt of her anger if it helped her to cope with her other problems, but to his surprise Granville spoke up.

'Don't blame Matthew,' he said levelly. 'He's a jailbird. Unlike Newman, he has no idea how a lawman's supposed to act, but Wyndham will find your son and your husband will be fine. Their fates are in the hands of people who know what they're doing.'

Abigail fought back the tears and

nodded to Granville before she shuffled back into the surgery. She didn't look at him again.

Anger at his father's comment rooted Matthew to the spot, but the decision as to whether he should stay was taken away from him when Hamilton took his arm.

'My patients need calm,' he said. He ushered him outside and Matthew didn't object. When they were in the corridor and beyond Granville's hearing, he continued. 'And I'm sure you can be better employed finding Jimmy.'

Matthew provided a thin smile. 'I'm pleased that someone has faith in me.'

'Wyndham's a good man. Follow his lead and one day you'll earn people's respect. As your father implied, being a lawman is as tough a job as being a doctor.'

Matthew nodded and, as Hamilton was one of the few people who hadn't treated him with contempt, when they were outside he turned to him.

'You're right,' he said. 'I keep being

told I need to behave like a lawman, except nobody's told me what that involves.'

'I'm sure you'll figure it out. Wyndham did, as did your brother.' Hamilton rocked his head from side to side. 'Wyndham always asks me plenty of questions.'

Matthew sighed and waved his arms vaguely while he wondered what Wyndham would ask if he were there.

'Did Franklin's injuries give you any ideas about who attacked him?' he asked.

'No,' Hamilton said.

The question had sounded a lame one to Matthew's ears, but Hamilton provided an encouraging smile and so he continued.

'Do you reckon his injuries all came from the fall?'

Hamilton raised an eyebrow. 'That's a good question. You're wondering if he knocked his head when he fell or if he was knocked on the head and then fell. Sadly, the answer is, I don't know.'

128

'But him falling off such a high bridge accidentally sounds unlikely. I've only been on it once and I stayed away from the edge . . . ' Matthew looked aloft as an obvious point hit him. His heart beat faster as he considered the matter in the way he reckoned Wyndham would want him to. 'Has anyone ever survived after falling off that bridge?'

'Not to my knowledge. Two workers fell off when they were building the bridge. One died instantly and the other was swept away never to be seen again. As I said, Franklin was lucky.'

'Or,' Matthew said, slapping Hamilton's shoulder and grinning, 'he didn't fall off the bridge.'

Thirty minutes later, Matthew stood on the railroad tracks before the bridge, as he had done the previous morning, except this time he had no choice but to look over the side at the dizzying scene below.

The snaking river filled most of the

gorge, but on this side the rocky base on which the bridge stanchions rested was wide enough to traverse on foot. Presumably this was where Wyndham had found Franklin and that meant there was a way down.

He started looking and, within a few minutes, found the paths that the workers must have carved out on either side of the bridge.

Matthew chose the downriver path, although it didn't appear to have been used recently. He reached the bottom in ten minutes and stood on the rocky ground peering up at the bridge that towered above him.

He tried to work out the highest point from which Franklin could have fallen from the structure and survived. He quickly dismissed that thought as there was no obvious reason why he would have been clambering around beneath the bridge.

He turned his attention on to the gorge. Carefully he picked his way around the boulders that were strewn beside the river while he peered up the steep side.

When he reached the second snaking path, his gaze locked on to the most likely place that Franklin might have been exploring when he fell.

A thick rope dangled from a flattened area close to the path. The flat area was a quarter of the way up the gorge and the rope reached all the way to the ground. Rusting machinery filled the flattened area suggesting that a winch had once been used to lower equipment and wood to the bottom.

Matthew moved on to stand beneath the rope from where he ran his gaze up to the path. The climb to reach the winch was around a hundred feet up a sheer expanse of rock. He considered the rock, noting indentations, several hollows and a cave at the halfway point.

'Is that what interested you?' Matthew murmured to himself and then, accepting there was only one way to answer his question, spat on his hands and put them to the rope.

The first few feet were the hardest to traverse. The rough rope was easy to grip, but Matthew struggled to work out how to raise himself.

After an aborted attempt in which, after much grunting and sweating, he climbed for only a few feet, he dropped back down to earth and reconsidered. A few minutes later, he worked out that leaning back and putting his feet to the rock worked best.

Effectively, walking upwards, he drew himself up. After twenty feet, the strain on his wrists made his arms feel as if they were being dragged from their sockets and so he sought out easier ways to climb.

Nothing worked any better than just moving one laboured pace at a time. So, with the thought looming that he could imagine how Franklin had come to harm, he sought out a ledge on which to rest.

As he approached the first suitable looking ledge, he was walking with his head pointing downwards and every dragged movement upwards felt as if it'd be the last he could manage.

With a sigh of relief, he placed his feet on the ledge, raised himself a little higher, and then hugged the rock as he gave his arms a welcome rest.

When he took stock of his position, he was embarrassed to find he had climbed only a third of the way up and his arms were shaking so violently he doubted he could explore the whole stretch. He leaned back and craned his neck.

The cave was ten feet above his head. The next landmark after that was several hollows situated further away than the distance he'd climbed already.

These observations restored his spirits as he reckoned that the cave was the highest point he could reach and, from here, the hollows didn't look interesting.

He finished off by running his gaze up to the winch. He flinched.

A man was peering down at him and, when that man noticed that he'd been seen, he held on to the rope and leaned over the edge. Matthew saw that it was Lawrence Deno.

'What are you looking for, Matthew?' Lawrence shouted with a mocking tone.

'Whatever you don't want me to find,' Matthew said.

Lawrence backed away from the edge. When he returned, he was holding a six-shooter, which he aimed down at him.

With both hands occupied, Matthew had no way to fight back and so he pressed his chest to the rock-face.

That movement took Lawrence out of his eyeline, with only the bumps in the rough rock above offering him protection. But when a gunshot blasted, it sliced shards from the rock only a foot from his face making him jerk his head away.

He hadn't thought that Lawrence could hit a spot that close to him and so he looked down at the ledge wondering where he could go to avoid the next shot. Then, with a lurch of his stomach, he saw the full extent of the peril he faced.

Below him, Abraham Deno was holstering his gun. He was making his way around the boulders, picking his route with care over a slippery patch. After another dozen paces he would be beneath him where, dangling thirty feet above his head, he would present an easy target.

In determination to avoid the fate that had presumably befallen Franklin of being shot at until he lost his balance, he concentrated on the only action open to him: reaching the cave.

He put both hands to the highest point on the rope he could reach and, with his legs bent, scurried upwards. Using frantic gestures, he tugged himself up while ensuring he placed his feet on every protuberance that would provide purchase.

Every time he gained a new hand-hold, he expected to feel a fatal shot tearing into his chest or back, but it didn't come and so he risked glancing down.

Abraham was standing directly below him, suggesting that neither man had fired again for fear of hitting the other. Abraham was gesturing at Lawrence to back away and so, figuring he had only a few moments left, Matthew abandoned caution.

He pushed out from the rock to stand with his legs extended and, with a shuffling walk, he dragged himself up. After two paces, the lip of the cave was four short paces away and he could see the roof and a darkened interior.

He took one pace and then another, the knowledge that he could rest soon letting him put all his energies into moving.

Then Abraham fired. The slug kicked dust from a ledge above the cave making Matthew think it must have missed him by inches.

Abraham would have him in his sights now and so to confuse his aim he bent his legs and moved closer to the wall. Then, with all his strength, he kicked off, pushing himself away from the rock so that he went swinging free.

A second wild shot came from below and, while swinging outwards, he saw Lawrence loitering close to the edge to watch his progress, sporting an incredulous expression. Then, on reaching the outermost extent of his swing, he went hurtling back towards the rock.

While still moving in, he clawed himself up hand over hand for another two feet. Then he raised his legs and, to his relief, they went swinging in through the cave entrance.

He released the rope and, for a terrible moment, he dropped. Then his legs slammed down inside the cave with the lip pressing into his back.

He floundered until, with a wave of his arms, he twisted his body and moved into a position where he could rest his chest on the base of the cave.

Then he rolled over and lay in the darkness breathing in a sigh of relief. He even smiled when he heard Abraham and Lawrence snapping angry recriminations at each other.

Quickly he shuffled up into a sitting position. With his back to the wall, he peered into the cave, seeking out what the Deno brothers were protecting.

At first, he could see only darkness, but then he saw movement. A few moments later his gaze focused on the boy sitting with his legs drawn up to his chest at the back of the cave.

'Jimmy?' he asked.

'I'm not answering no questions until I see my mother,' the boy said, raising his small fists in defiance.

'Then,' Matthew said with a smile, 'I'll try not to keep you waiting for long.'

10

'My mother says I shouldn't speak to men I don't know,' Jimmy said.

He shuffled backwards for another foot into the cave until he pressed himself into the corner, but he still kept his fists raised and so Matthew backed away to the cave entrance to avoid unduly worrying him.

'That shouldn't include me,' he said. 'You saw me in the hotel yesterday when I was helping Marshal Wyndham look for your father's stolen money.'

Jimmy nodded and after a moment's thought, he lowered his fists.

'What are you doing now?'

'I was looking for you. Now that I've found you, I'll help you.'

'I don't need your help. My father will find me.'

This disturbing comment made Matthew gulp, but he consoled himself with the thought that this meant Jimmy hadn't seen Franklin get injured.

'When I spoke with him, he was very worried about you. He won't mind who finds you as long as you're safe.'

The mention of danger made Jimmy frown and, as Matthew couldn't think of any soothing words, he risked glancing through the entrance.

Below, Abraham was looking at the river with a foot raised on a rock, his casual posture suggesting that he wasn't concerned that Matthew had escaped, presumably because he was now trapped.

'What's a rancid son of a bitch?' Jimmy asked.

Matthew started and then turned back.

'You shouldn't say such things. Where did you hear that?'

'My mother said that to my father when they were talking about you. They thought I couldn't hear, but I did.'

Matthew shuffled away from the entrance as he struggled to find an answer.

'It means your mother wasn't happy with me.'

'Why?'

'Because . . . ' Matthew rocked his head from side to side and then settled for a believable lie. 'Because I accused one of the hotel guests of stealing the money.'

'Why did you do that?'

'I reckoned he was acting suspiciously, but I got it wrong.'

'What was he doing?'

'He was in his room in the early afternoon.'

'Why was he there?'

Matthew rubbed his forehead, the constant questions giving him a twinge of a headache.

'You sure have got plenty of questions.'

'Have I?'

Matthew winced. 'Jimmy, it's not important what we argued about. All that matters is that your mother wasn't happy with me, but she will be when she finds out how happy you are that

I've found you.'

Jimmy jutted his jaw while he considered this answer and, presumably because it didn't lend itself to another question, he contented himself with a nod. Then he shuffled towards the entrance.

'I'm hungry and I'm thirsty.'

'Didn't they leave you with anything?'

'No.' Jimmy sat opposite him. 'Why are you allowed to ask questions when I'm not?'

Matthew sighed. 'Because that's my job.'

Jimmy laughed, his understanding smile making him look older than his years and, with him sitting in the full light for the first time, Matthew couldn't help but examine his features closely.

Then he shook his head, reminding himself of his promise not to dwell on the matter. Instead, he put his mind to the problem of their escape.

The sun was close to the corner post

of the bridge and it would disappear from view within the hour after which it would get dark in little more than another hour.

Sneaking out of the cave, down the rope, and then past the Deno brothers would be tricky on his own, but in the dark with Jimmy in tow, it could be impossible.

'You won't leave me here, will you?' Jimmy said, his voice small as he searched Matthew's eyes.

'I won't,' Matthew said, although he couldn't see how he could fulfil his promise.

Jimmy smiled and, seeing that an obvious question was on his lips, Matthew checked on the rope that he would have to climb down in the dark.

He leaned forward until Abraham came into view. He was standing on the edge of the water where he had a good view of the cave while Lawrence was making his way towards him.

'It's a long climb down, and that kid's heavy,' Abraham called. Ruefully he rubbed a shoulder. 'You try to get him down and he could drop like a stone.'

'We're comfortable up here,' Matthew called back, speaking quickly before Abraham got a chance to taunt him about Franklin's fate, 'and we can hold you off for as long as we want to.'

'Then do that. We don't aim to keep you there for ever.' Abraham waited until Lawrence was standing beside him. 'Noon tomorrow and, if your father doesn't stand for mayor, you can go.'

'Or at least one of you can,' Lawrence added.

'You'll need a second plan. When I left town, Granville was still planning to stand. He said he'll never give in to threats from people like you.'

'And your father, a man who won't even look at you, told you that, did he?'

Abraham waited for an answer. When Matthew couldn't provide one, he waved a dismissive hand at him. Then he and Lawrence settled down on a flat boulder to watch the cave and chat.

Their arrogant attitudes gave Matthew no confidence that they'd honour their promise not to endanger Jimmy if they stayed where they were, so he knelt down, facing the boy.

'We wait until dark,' he said. 'Then we leave. And I'll need your help.'

'What do you want me to do?' Jimmy murmured uncertainly.

As Jimmy sported a dubious expression and he hadn't worked out all the details of their escape plan yet, Matthew ventured a smile and then unhooked the star from his chest.

'You like asking questions and that's what good lawmen do.' He pinned the star on Jimmy's jacket. 'I'm a deputy and now I've appointed you as my deputy.'

Jimmy happily drew out his jacket to look at the star.

'What does a deputy's deputy do?'

'The first thing a deputy's deputy does,' Matthew said with a wink, making Jimmy giggle, 'is to stay quiet.

Then he goes to sleep.'

Jimmy considered and then lay on his side.

'How quiet?' he asked. 'And how fast does he — ?'

Matthew put a finger to his lips and then placed his hands beside his head in an attitude of sleep.

'A deputy does as he's told.'

'Does that mean you do as you're told?'

Matthew sighed. 'This is going to be a long night.'

★　★　★

Low moonlight was making small bows of light dance on the river when Matthew looked out of the cave entrance. Even better, the light had yet to reach the cave and so the rope was in darkness.

Earlier he'd decided to maximize their chances by waiting long into the night. While he'd still had the light, he'd browsed through the journal that Elijah

Moon had secreted away in his bottom drawer.

Unfortunately, the incriminating evidence he had hoped to find wasn't immediately obvious.

The journal merely listed names and numbers. The light had been fading when Matthew had started to spot recurring names, but he didn't recognize any of them.

He decided that the numbers were probably bribes, both received and given. The most regular payments were to a man called Hilderic Rainhart, a name that meant nothing to Matthew. The last two amounts were detailed as being made to him, although they had been crossed out.

With the unresolved implications of this discovery on his mind, he'd joined Jimmy in sleeping on the hard floor of the cave.

Now, his plan appeared to have worked well as he could see the sleeping form of one of their guards lying on the flat rock beside the river. He couldn't discern which one of the brothers it was and neither could he see the second brother.

But the dead of night was the time when they should be at their least alert, and Matthew didn't plan to go where he would be expected to go.

He shook Jimmy's shoulder and, thankfully, the boy only murmured sleepily before he came awake. He sat up, stretched, and then started to lie down again.

'Jimmy,' Matthew whispered. 'It's time now to take you back to your mother and father.'

'I'm tired. Can't I stay here?'

'You're a deputy now.' Matthew tapped the star on the boy's chest. 'Remember, you have to do as you're told.'

'But I'm tired. Do I have to be a deputy any more?'

Matthew gritted his teeth, lost for the right thing to say when he had no experience of dealing with children. He placed both hands on Jimmy's shoulders.

'You do because deputies get to play games, and tonight we're going to sneak out of the cave without being seen or heard.' Matthew raised his tone slightly to make the endeavour sound fun, but Jimmy only shrugged. 'Haven't you tried to sneak away from home at night without your parents noticing before?'

'No. They wouldn't want me to do that.'

'It must have been just me, then,' Matthew murmured to himself. He gave Jimmy a nudge towards the cave entrance. 'Come on. Do this one thing and then you can go back to sleep.'

Jimmy yawned, but he provided a tired nod and, with that reaction being the best he could hope for, Matthew set about carrying out his plan. He removed his belt and looped it around his neck and beneath an arm.

Thankfully, Jimmy was thin and he was able to wrap the belt around his chest. It wouldn't be strong enough to support him, but with some help from the boy, he reckoned that in a tricky situation, it would help him avoid disaster.

Jimmy was still half-asleep and docile, so he limited his instructions to telling him to keep a tight grip of his shoulders. Then he moved to the cave entrance and, before doubts assailed him, he grabbed the rope and stood up.

His assumption was that the Deno brothers were taking it in turns to sleep while the other guarded the bottom. Therefore, he drew himself up and embarked on the fifty-foot expedition to the winch above, a journey that felt as if it'd be longer than the ten-mile walk to town would be.

To his delight, despite the extra weight, he made quick progress. The different climbing methods he'd tried earlier had helped him to find an efficient way to climb and, within a minute, he saw the outline of the winch above him in the dark.

Jimmy had locked his arms around his shoulders and he was breathing quietly. Matthew was grateful for this

150

and he moved on hoping to reach the top before he had to take a rest or Jimmy became fully aware of what was happening.

He was ten feet from the top when his biceps cramped forcing him to place his feet in a hollow while he flexed his arms. The delay gave him time to look around.

The winch above appeared un-guarded and, when he looked down, the form of the sleeping man hadn't moved. The moon had now drifted further across the sky illuminating most of the ground beside the river, but the other guard still wasn't visible.

'Are we there yet?' Jimmy murmured with a tired shrug. 'I want to sleep.'

'Shut up, kid, and stay still,' Matthew muttered, finally losing patience and, with his irritated mood giving him a burst of strength, he yanked himself up.

With five brisk hand-over-hand motions, he got first one foot and then his other knee up to the lip of the rock. Another tug got him into a position where he could swing Jimmy round and set him down on the ledge.

The reduction in weight let him readily manoeuvre himself on to the ledge beside the winch where he rolled them both over and away from the edge. On his back he caught his breath with Jimmy clutched to his side.

'I'm awake now,' Jimmy said, poking him in the ribs. 'Why are you lying around?'

Matthew patted his shoulder. Then he detached them and checked the flat area.

The moonlight was strong enough to confirm that nobody was there, so he took Jimmy's hand and led him to the snaking path up the side of the gorge.

In the moonlight, they made slow and careful progress until the path brought them out before the bridge.

Matthew had expected the Deno brothers to have taken his horse from where he'd tethered it to the fence that led on to the bridge, so he wasn't disappointed when he confirmed his fear. With a last encouraging pat on the back for Jimmy, he headed into the centre of the tracks and turned towards town.

Lawrence was standing twenty feet down the tracks with his gun already aimed at them.

'Now,' he said, 'where do you two think you're going?'

11

Matthew wasn't convinced that Lawrence wouldn't harm the boy and so he grabbed Jimmy's shoulders, turned him around, and hurried away.

They reached the path leading back down into the gorge, but they'd run on for only a few paces when Abraham came into view thirty feet away, striding purposefully towards them with his gun drawn.

'It must be tough for you,' he said, 'to find that all your climbing was for nothing.'

In the poor light and on his own, Matthew reckoned he might get lucky in a gunfight, but he couldn't endanger Jimmy and so he wrapped an arm around his shoulders and retreated. Unfortunately, with Lawrence guarding the route towards town, he had no choice but to head on to the bridge.

When the brothers didn't object, he carried on down the centre of the tracks. A quarter of the way across he stopped.

He placed Jimmy behind his back and turned to face the end of the bridge. Abraham and Lawrence had moved on to stand on either side of the tracks facing him.

'Keep on going,' Lawrence said, gesturing at him with his gun. 'You don't want to risk the kid's life.'

With an irritated shake of his head, Matthew did as he'd been ordered. He turned his back on the men and ushered Jimmy to move on, which he did without complaint.

Only when they reached the other side did he look back again. His adversaries had stayed on the opposite side of the gorge, but with this being the only way across the river for dozens of miles in either direction, they didn't need to follow them.

He and Jimmy settled down sitting on a track close to the bridge but away from the edge.

'Does this mean you're not taking me home now?' Jimmy asked after a while.

'I will, but later,' Matthew said. He considered the lightening horizon. 'When those men have gone away.'

'But they won't go, will they?'

'They won't. But there's plenty of time for the unexpected to happen.' Matthew started to provide a comforting smile, but then Jimmy opened his mouth and so he spoke quickly. 'And before you ask, I don't know what unexpected things might happen, and I don't have any ideas about how we can get across the gorge.'

Matthew stood up and moved away from the tracks, partially to get a better view across the gorge but mainly to get a few moments of peace so he could think. Jimmy followed him and waited until he'd considered the bridge.

'I know,' he said, shuffling from side to side as he peered past him at the gorge, 'that deputies have to be quiet and follow orders.'

'They do,' Matthew said wearily.

'But can they come up with ideas too?'

'They can.' Matthew lowered himself to Jimmy's eyeline. 'Do you have a plan, Deputy?'

'I sure do.' Jimmy pointed down into the gorge. 'We go down the side of the gorge and then we walk along those planks under the bridge to reach the other side.'

Matthew winced, having already dismissed that idea as being too reckless, but with Jimmy looking eager and unworried after he'd offered his idea, he didn't want to disappoint him.

'Let's see if it'll work, then,' he said.

Although the light level was still too low to see clearly across the gorge, he took Jimmy down the tracks. Then they doubled back, coming out at a point that he'd seen earlier where the slope down into the gorge wasn't as steep as elsewhere.

The slope let them slip under the bridge where they were able to rest against a stanchion and await the arrival of better light.

The timbers on which they'd have to cross the gorge were three feet wide, which Matthew reckoned was wide enough to walk with ease. But when the sun rose and lit up the bridge, he decided that waiting for the light had been a bad idea as he could see what was below.

'I want to go home,' Jimmy said. 'When are we going across?'

Matthew sighed. The drop down to the water was several times longer than the climb he'd completed in the dark. As his adversaries' plan was to keep them away from town until noon, he judged that he couldn't risk Jimmy's life.

'I'm sorry, but we're not going across.' When Jimmy started pouting and complaining, Matthew searched for a good excuse and then settled for the truth. 'It's too dangerous.'

Jimmy peered down at the water thundering by hundreds of feet below, all moiling and foam-flecked.

'Are you scared of heights?'

'Yeah. And you?'

'No.'

Jimmy provided a wicked smile. Then he stood up quickly and leapt on to the nearest timber.

'Stop right there,' Matthew urged. With his arms held out, he moved forward while still staying on the ground.

Jimmy turned to him and, with his hands on his hips, he danced from foot to foot to show how easy it was to walk on the struts.

'You can't tell me what to do,' he said. 'You're not my father.'

Matthew gulped. 'Maybe I'm not, but you're my deputy.'

Jimmy bit his lip as he considered. Then, with a determined swing of the shoulders, he turned round, held his arms out to either side, and walked carefully forward.

Within seconds he had moved out to a point where a fall would seriously injure him. Matthew reckoned he could follow and scoop him up, but instead, with a shake of the head, he decided to support his reckless plan.

He adopted Jimmy's posture of holding his arms out and paced along behind him, keeping a distance that was far enough away not to hinder the boy but close enough to grab him if he got into difficulty. Fifty feet on, Jimmy stopped at the first stanchion and waited for him.

Jimmy's jaw was set firmly, but his darting eyes betrayed his growing fear, and so he didn't complain when Matthew manoeuvred himself past him. Then Matthew directed him to grab hold of the back of his jacket and, in tandem, they continued on across the bridge.

With his thoughts centred on keeping Jimmy's fears at bay, Matthew didn't find the experience as disconcerting as when he'd first walked on to the bridge two days before. So, using short journeys between each stanchion, they

160

gradually worked their way across.

Matthew didn't like to contemplate the possibility that the Deno brothers were aware of their escape attempt, but he was heartened that he didn't see any sign of them until they reached the last stretch.

Through gaps in the wood above, he saw Lawrence walking back and forth across the bridge with a bored tread.

For several minutes, Matthew waited in the hope that this time he could confirm where Abraham was, but he didn't appear and so, after giving Jimmy a comforting smile, he set off.

Unlike on the opposite side of the gorge, the slope on this side was steep and Matthew reckoned they'd have to clamber on hands and feet beside the final stanchion to reach the top. Worse, thirty yards away from the bridge the slope became sheer and so the only route they could take would bring them out in full view of their guards.

But this time they'd have the element of surprise and so, the moment he reached the end of the timber path, he turned to Jimmy planning to urge him to stay put while he dealt with the brothers.

He had yet to find a way to explain himself quietly when Jimmy's eyes opened wide and he pointed over Matthew's shoulder.

Matthew swirled round to find that Abraham was stepping out from behind the final stanchion five yards away. Matthew spread his arms seeking to shield Jimmy while also taking a long step forward. The quick action unbalanced him.

He went to one knee on the edge of the timber where he stared down the steep slope that promised a long and fatal tumble to the rocks below. By the time he'd stilled himself, Abraham had come on to the strut, but he kept back, his gaze as uncertain as Matthew's had been when he'd first stepped on to a strut.

The long journey across the gorge had increased Matthew's confidence and the moment he was sure that Abraham wouldn't come any further forward, he leapt up.

With a shoulder thrust down, he charged him. He pounded on for three paces until he hit Abraham in the stomach.

His momentum carried him on for a pace until Abraham slipped. His foot went over the side and, with a frantic wide-eyed expression on his face, he wheeled his arms.

A strangulated cry escaped Abraham's lips as he fell backwards and landed on the sloping ground.

Then Matthew had problems of his own to deal with as his momentum kept him moving on for two more paces until he stopped himself with his hands against the slope. He hugged the earth with relief until he was sure that he wouldn't slip.

'Watch out!' Jimmy shouted behind him.

Matthew glanced down expecting to see that Abraham was climbing back up, but he had only managed to grab hold of a bush. He was making its precarious hold on the side even more precarious as he tried to claw his way past it.

A solid blow slammed into Matthew's shoulders from above, knocking him down on to both knees. He registered a moment later that Jimmy had been warning him about Lawrence, who had taken the reckless action of sliding down the slope.

A second blow in the middle of the back flattened him to the wood. Then Lawrence thrust his boot under his chest and flipped him over.

Matthew tumbled over the side. For a gut-wrenching moment, the rocks below beckoned him on until, with a desperate lunge, he clawed at the wood.

His fingers jammed into a split in the wood and halted his fall. When he took stock of his situation, one arm and one leg were dangling over the side, and his other leg was pressed to the edge.

He looked up and, with relief, he saw that his adversary had moved on, although his stomach lurched when he saw that Lawrence was advancing on Jimmy with his arms spread, ready to gather him up.

Matthew dragged his dangling leg up on to the timber as Lawrence reached the boy, who proved he was his mother's son by kicking Lawrence's ankle, making him curse and hop away.

Jimmy followed through with his head down and his small fists whirling. This onslaught was easier to fend off, but Lawrence didn't get the chance.

His second hop landed him on the edge of the timber. Then, with a pained screech and a frantic lunge in the opposite direction that failed to help him keep his balance, he tipped over the side.

He had been standing further out than Abraham had been and he dropped for twenty feet before he crashed headfirst into the slope. Then he rebounded out over a sheer stretch where there was nothing below to cushion his fall other than the rocks at the bottom of the gorge.

A desperate cry that faded quickly rent the air. By the time Matthew had reached Jimmy and he was holding him tightly, the cry had cut off.

'Are you all right?' Matthew asked.

'I killed a man,' Jimmy whined against his chest. 'I punched him so hard he went flying over the edge.'

'You didn't,' Matthew said, keeping his tone as light as he could manage. 'You kicked Lawrence and that hurt him. He moved out of your way, but then he tripped and fell over the edge.'

'He still got killed.'

'He didn't. I saw him limping away down there and he'll be fine when his brother climbs down to look after him.'

Matthew then manoeuvred Jimmy along the strut while keeping his head raised so that he couldn't look down and see that he'd lied.

'Should we go down,' Jimmy said when they reached the slope, 'and make sure he'll be all right?'

'No. He'll be mad at us.'

'I guess so,' Jimmy said. He moved away to look him in the eye and for once Matthew didn't mind getting asked another question. 'Is that what really happened?'

'Sure.' Matthew glanced down at Abraham who was struggling to gather a firm handhold and so avoid joining Lawrence in the quick and fatal journey down to the bottom of the gorge. 'But it'd be best not to tell your mother about this. She won't understand, so it can be our secret.'

To stop Jimmy asking him any more questions, he ushered him to move up the slope ahead of him. When they'd clambered up to the bridge and were facing the railroad tracks that led on to Snake Ridge, Jimmy turned to him.

'I won't tell her,' he said, 'but I'll tell my father. He'll understand.'

'He sure does,' Matthew murmured to himself.

12

It was mid-morning when Matthew rode back into town with Jimmy sitting before him.

Earlier, they had located his horse. Then they had run off Abraham's and Lawrence's steeds to delay Abraham if he managed to climb back up to the bridge.

Jimmy had been quiet, and Matthew was unsure whether his failure to question the version of events he had told him was a good sign or a bad one.

He headed to the Hotel Splendour, judging that even if Abigail wasn't there, someone could look after the boy, but as it turned out Abigail was on duty at the reception desk. Her glassy-eyed, stoic expression showed that she was struggling to carry on as if everything was normal, and so Matthew was halfway across the room before she registered he'd come in.

Jimmy was walking stiff-legged and shocked while clutching him. When he saw Abigail, he gave up the brave act he'd been putting on and sobbed while hurrying forward with his arms thrust out.

As soon as he was in her arms, Matthew turned away. He'd reached the door when she spoke up.

'Thank you,' she said.

He turned and offered her a quick smile, but took the sensible option of saying nothing, relieved that if they never spoke again, he could at least claim he'd righted one wrong in Snake Ridge. He glanced at Jimmy, pleased that, whatever the truth about him, he'd spent time with him.

Then, before she took umbrage at him looking at her son, he left. His first visit was to the surgery where he learnt that his father had returned to his cell, bruised but otherwise fine. Franklin had regained consciousness although he was resting and not seeing visitors.

The doctor was more optimistic about his chances than he had been the day before and he promised to pass on the good news about Jimmy. Then Matthew moved on to the law office, reckoning that his run of people who had been delighted to see him was about to end.

He was right.

'You've been gone for nearly a whole day,' Wyndham said, standing in the middle of the office looking weary and bow-backed. 'If you don't want me to carry out Elijah Moon's threat for him, you'd better make your next words mighty fine ones.'

'I found Jimmy,' Matthew said. 'He's with his mother now. He's fine.'

'Where did you find him?' Wyndham said, his gruff voice showing that he wasn't ready to forgive him immediately.

Matthew went on to detail the events since they'd last seen each other. During his tale, Wyndham gradually relaxed and began nodding.

'Lawrence Deno then attacked us,' Matthew said finishing off his explanation with the version of events he'd decided to offer as the official one, 'but he lost his footing and he fell off the bridge.'

'I can't say I'm sorry to hear about his demise,' Wyndham said. 'I'm more worried about the effect it'll have on Jimmy. It can't have done him much good to see that happen after being kidnapped and held hostage overnight.'

'He's with his mother. She'll look after him, and it'll help even more if we can enjoy a peaceful time from now on.' Matthew considered Wyndham's frown. 'So what happened here last night?'

'It was quiet, surprisingly.' Wyndham raised his hat to run fingers through his hair. 'While you were finding Jimmy, I followed Elijah. He met this other man. They talked and I assume they had a change of heart because the trouble I expected never erupted, which I'm thankful for, seeing as how I was on my own.'

'I'm sorry.' Matthew provided an apologetic smile, and Wyndham took the opportunity to return it.

'I was cursing you last night, but I guess I did want a deputy with initiative.' Wyndham glanced at the clock that showed they had ninety minutes before the noon deadline. He gestured at the jailhouse. 'Come on, let's get your father to the mayor's office early.'

Fifteen minutes later, the three men were sitting in the main office upstairs. Matthew didn't know what to expect of the process of registering the applications to become the next mayor, but it turned out to be a mundane one.

Granville placed an official looking parchment in the middle of the desk and then turned away from him. At the top was his short statement that the undersigned wished to tender their names and at the bottom lay a pen.

After noon, the document would be posted outside. Granville didn't sign it himself; instead he sat back in his chair with his arms folded. Throughout the process, he had remained silent and for the next ten minutes the three men took his lead in keeping quiet.

Five minutes before eleven, the first signs of activity came when the door downstairs opened. The arrivals were Elijah Moon and Abraham Deno.

Elijah wasn't as surly as he had been when he'd last seen him while Abraham looked shocked. They walked quietly across the office and took up positions sitting in chairs by the window. Elijah stared at the door while Abraham glared thunderously across the office at Matthew.

The clock behind the mayor's desk tinkled the hour, breaking the silent tension. Elijah turned to Granville.

'Have you signed?' he asked.

'I haven't,' Granville said, his voice croaking after his lengthy silence. He considered Elijah for a while. 'Will you?'

'I won't. I've only come to see who does sign.'

Granville gave a slow nod and then returned to looking at the document, as if this decision wasn't a surprise. Wyndham and Matthew exchanged bemused glances before Wyndham asked the obvious question.

'You mean after all the mayhem of the last few days,' he said, 'neither of you are standing?'

Granville moved the pen a few inches to lie beside the document.

'I'm facing charges,' he said, 'of stealing money from my good friend Franklin Buxton and of murdering my beloved son. It's not appropriate for me to consider being the next mayor.'

Wyndham turned to Elijah. 'And it's sure not appropriate for you to stand because once I've pieced together everything that's happened here, you'll be facing charges, starting with kidnapping a child.'

'Do your worst, lawman,' Elijah said with a bored tone.

Wyndham narrowed his eyes. 'Except you'd have known that'd be my reaction when you started your campaign of intimidation against Franklin and Granville. So why back out now?'

'Now is not the right time for me either,' Elijah said. 'But either way, nobody will back up your allegations.'

Wyndham looked from one man to the other, shaking his head in bemusement.

'A deal's been done here,' he declared.

Wyndham waited, but Granville kept his head lowered and Elijah wouldn't meet his eye.

'You don't know nothing, lawman,' Elijah said as the door creaked open downstairs.

With Elijah and Granville saying nothing more, they listened to a man walking up the stairs.

'Some of your charges can be defeated with silence,' Wyndham said, waving a finger at Elijah, 'but I'll get to the truth about the death of Newman Jennings and the attack on Franklin Buxton.'

'Do your duty,' Elijah said without concern as he looked at the door, 'while we work to pull this town together.'

'But under who?' Wyndham waited for an answer, but when neither man replied, he persisted. 'Who will be the new mayor?'

'I will,' the newcomer said from the doorway.

The voice had been familiar and, when the man stepped forward, Matthew winced as he got his first proper sighting of his secretive adversary.

The man gave Matthew an amused sideways glance before nodding to both Elijah and Granville. Then he headed over to the desk and picked up the pen.

'You're the man Elijah met at Hunter's Pass yesterday,' Wyndham said. 'Who are you?'

'He's Hilderic Rainhart,' Matthew said.

Wyndham rounded on him. 'How do you know that?'

Matthew couldn't think of a suitable reply and so he watched Hilderic sign

176

the document with a flourish.

'I believe he's been thinking,' Hilderic said, turning from the desk, 'which is a good thing for a lawman to do. If the previous marshal of Snake Ridge had done his job properly, this could all have been avoided.'

'Newman Jennings was the lawman before me.' Wyndham looked aloft and then nodded. 'And Hilderic Rainhart was the outlaw he arrested for robbing the bank here ten years ago.'

Matthew was relieved that Wyndham was looking at Hilderic, and so he didn't see him flinch.

'I got eight years,' Hilderic said. 'But thankfully Snake Ridge is a forgiving town. It doesn't mind having a former jailbird as a lawman and so I'm sure it won't mind having a former jailbird as mayor.'

He turned to Matthew. For long moments the two men locked gazes. Then, with a smile on his lips, Hilderic headed back to the door.

Nobody spoke as he paced out of the

room and down the stairs. Only when the main door rattled did Wyndham break the silence.

'All the time I thought the battle being fought here was between you and Franklin,' he said, looking at Elijah, 'but in reality it was between you and Hilderic.'

'You'll never figure it all out,' Elijah said.

Wyndham turned to Matthew. 'Stay here until noon. I'll see what else I can learn about Hilderic Rainhart.'

Wyndham hurried from the room leaving the remaining men to sit in silence for several minutes until Elijah stood up. He paced slowly across the office with Abraham at his shoulder.

'Make your peace with your father, Matthew,' he said. He glanced at the clock. 'You have fifty minutes.'

'Don't threaten a lawman,' Matthew said, 'who's going nowhere.'

'I'm not threatening you. I'm warning you that I know what you did yesterday in my hotel.'

Matthew gulped. 'And after what I learnt in your hotel yesterday, I know what you've been doing.'

'Except you won't get the chance to use that information. Hilderic spent eight years in jail for a crime he didn't commit. He wants revenge. I placated him with money. Your only way to placate him is with blood.' Elijah chuckled. 'I did try to warn you.'

Elijah moved towards the door, leaving Abraham to glare at him.

'And,' he said, 'I'll grind whatever Hilderic leaves behind into the dirt until your battered hide looks like Lawrence's body.'

Matthew didn't reply to the threats other than to return both men's glares. Then he watched them leave. When the door had been slammed shut, he turned to Granville.

'It seems everyone wants me dead,' he said. 'So have you got any last words to say to your son?'

Granville looked at him, this being the biggest reaction he'd provided since he'd last spoken to him two days before, but he said nothing.

'Not even,' Matthew persisted, 'to provide an explanation of why you backed out of becoming mayor in favour of a man who wants to kill me?'

Granville tensed his jaw and then looked down at the document. He even turned it round to read the one name there, and Matthew had become so adept at reading his father's silences that he could tell he was reaching breaking point.

'So,' Matthew said, 'if nobody else has the guts to stand up to Hilderic, I'll have to do it.'

He headed to the desk and drew the document closer. He read the declaration, making Granville breathe deeply. Then he reached for the pen.

With an unthinking reaction Granville slammed his hand down over the pen before Matthew could touch it.

'You're not fit for this office,' Granville muttered, 'or for any other office that your brother filled with distinction.'

'A man like Hilderic,' Matthew said, biting back his surprise at getting him to speak, 'shouldn't become the next mayor unopposed.'

'He shouldn't, but you're not the man to oppose him.'

'That's not your decision.'

The end of the pen was poking out from under Granville's palm and Matthew moved for it. With a snarl, Granville scraped the pen away. Then, with his eyes blazing, he swirled the document around and signed with a quick movement before hurling the pen away.

He stared defiantly up at Matthew until, with a slight lowering of the eyelids, he conceded that he'd done exactly what Matthew had wanted him to do.

'Damn you,' he muttered.

'So now that you've proved you have got the guts to stand, tell me the — '

'I always could have done,' Granville

roared, leaping to his feet. 'But I was protecting you!'

In a moment the anger drained from Granville's expression and he flopped back down into his chair to stare at the document.

'How?' Matthew said.

Granville didn't reply for over a minute and when he did his voice was small.

'As I told you in the jailhouse, I have no answers for a man who's living a lie.'

Matthew sighed and, even though Granville wasn't looking at him, he turned away to look through the window.

'Ten years ago Elijah Moon, myself and two other men raided Snake Ridge's bank.' Matthew took a deep breath and, as Granville was keeping silent, he assumed he was making the confession his father wanted to hear. 'Nobody ever suspected it was us, but I now gather Hilderic Rainhart was arrested for the crime.'

'Hilderic was a lowlife gunslinger

who committed numerous local robberies. Newman had just been appointed marshal and he made enough connections to think him guilty.'

'And ten years later, Hilderic has returned to get revenge on the men who wronged him. He extorted money from Elijah and I assume he killed my brother.' Matthew waited, but Granville didn't reply. 'Then he blackmailed you and you tried to repay him with Franklin's money.'

Matthew turned to consider Granville, who was contemplating his shaking hands. For the first time he reckoned his father looked old.

'Hilderic blackmailed me to keep my family's shame secret,' Granville whispered. 'You can keep that secret by walking out of this room and never returning.'

'I can do that easily,' Matthew said. He turned to the door. 'One way or the other.'

13

Forty minutes before his noon deadline expired, Matthew stepped out on to the boardwalk.

Nobody was looking his way. So, not knowing when and where Hilderic would make his move, he decided to pre-empt him. He could think of only one place where Hilderic might go.

On his first night in Snake Ridge, he'd seen him standing outside a mercantile. That business had been built on the spot where the bank had once stood and, two nights before, it had been the scene of a battle between the owner and a gang of Elijah Moon's men.

When Matthew arrived, the building had been abandoned. The damage Elijah's club-wielding men had caused had been extensive and afterwards any remaining intact stock had been spirited away.

Matthew slipped in past the dangling broken panes of glass in the window and then picked his way through the debris to the middle of the room. The crunch of spilled corn that had been sprayed around the room accompanied every pace.

He presumed that the battle in here had taken place because the owner had given Hilderic a place to stay, but that didn't mean he would return.

Either way, he judged it a decent place to wait for the deadline to expire, and so he located the broken half of the counter and laid it over two crates. Then he sat facing the window.

Ten minutes later, behind him a crunched footfall sounded. He didn't turn. He waited for a second crunch before he spoke.

'You're early, Hilderic,' he said.

'I'm not Hilderic,' Creighton Kendrick said.

The unexpected answer made Matthew turn. Both Creighton and Tarrant had returned, although they both sported sour expressions.

'It seems,' Matthew said with a smile that neither man returned, 'that you had the same idea as I had.'

'That we *all* had,' a voice said from the back of the store.

When Matthew looked past Creighton, he saw that Hilderic was walking behind them and that he was escorting them in at gunpoint. Two hired guns flanked him, both with weapons already drawn.

'We stayed in town to help you,' Tarrant said with an apologetic frown. 'But he found us.'

Matthew stood up. 'Don't worry. It's appropriate that we four should end this together.'

'In which case Elijah should be here,' Tarrant grumbled.

Matthew waited for Hilderic to explain why that wouldn't happen, but he and his silent associates moved on until they were standing five feet behind the two men with one gun trained on each of them.

'Elijah and Hilderic did a deal,' Matthew said. 'Elijah bought his way out of getting what he deserved.'

Matthew glanced at Tarrant and Creighton, encouraging them to make the obvious offer, but Hilderic spoke up.

'I don't want the money you stole off Elijah,' he said. 'I got what I wanted from him.'

Hilderic smirked with a look that promised he'd already decided on the revenge he wanted to get from them. Matthew's concern must have been obvious as Creighton and Tarrant both reacted at the same time.

Creighton leapt to the left while Tarrant swirled round to face Hilderic. That sealed his fate when Hilderic and his two associates turned their guns on him instead of the other armed men.

They fired and rapid gunshots tore into Tarrant's side making him drop. Then, while his associates followed Creighton, with a snap of the wrist,

Hilderic swung his gun towards Matthew, but Matthew had already followed Creighton's lead in leaping to the side.

Matthew crashed down amidst the debris of the ruined stock. Two quick gunshots sounded. One slug tore into the crate to his side and then a moment later one of the hired guns staggered into view.

Matthew swung his gun up to aim at him, but he stilled his fire when he saw he'd been shot in the neck, presumably by Creighton before he went to ground. As the man toppled over without uttering a word, Matthew welcomed sinking down into the broken wood and strewn sacks.

He burrowed along like a snake until he gained the more substantial cover of his makeshift seat. Then, with his gun drawn, he glanced around the store.

Creighton, Hilderic and the last hired gun weren't visible. The only sign of life he could hear was Tarrant's ragged breathing nearby.

'We're even now,' Matthew called. 'Do you want to get them, Creighton? Or are you leaving them to me?'

'Hilderic's got even less fight in him than he had in the mayor's office,' Creighton shouted. 'I reckon he'll run away again. What do you reckon, Tarrant?'

This last attempt at bravado proved to be one taunt too many as Tarrant didn't reply, but the exchange told Matthew that Creighton was hiding behind a tipped over cupboard. Unfortunately, Hilderic and his associate didn't join in the taunting and so reveal where they were hiding.

So Matthew listened. With so much debris lying around it was impossible to move quietly and, sure enough, beyond the seat he heard rustling as someone tried to sneak up on him.

He trained his gun on a spot above the counter where he expected his opponent to appear. Silence dragged on for a minute. But, when he saw movement, it was from the corner of his eye and it came from four feet to the right of the earlier noise.

A gun appeared above a sack and then swung down as the hired gun planned to fire blindly. With only a moment to act, Matthew rolled over on to his back. His quick action saved him from a speculative gunshot that tore out and slammed into the floor.

He came to rest beneath the man's arm. He grabbed the wrist and thrust the arm up straight, the action loosing out another gunshot into the roof. Then he turned the tables on his assailant by swinging his own gun over the sack and firing blind.

He had a better idea of where the man was hiding and an agonized screech sounded. The arm went limp and the man slumped against the sack toppling it over to reveal his dying form.

Beyond him, lying amidst the heaps of broken furniture and damaged stock, was Tarrant. His breathing was shallow and he clutched his bleeding side. Then a pained grimace contorted his face and he arched his back before flopping back down.

Matthew watched him, but he didn't move again. That sight, on top of all the other recent incidents, sent a flurry of anger ripping through his guts.

He leapt to his feet. Standing up, he glimpsed Hilderic's hat ten feet away as he crouched down between a pile of leaking corn sacks and the wall.

Despite getting confirmation of their adversary's location, anger still drove him to jump up onto the counter. He aimed down at the hat, but he stilled his fire as he waited for Hilderic to move fully into view.

Instead, Hilderic ducked down, but Matthew had become familiar with the way he thought and so he trained his gun along the top of the sacks to a point four feet away from his original hiding place. He waited, and sure enough, a faint shadow moving across the wall heralded Hilderic's next action.

Matthew tensed, planning to fire the moment he appeared, but he must have shifted his weight as the counter beneath his feet rattled. Then it tipped over, spilling him forward.

With no control over his motion, he fell. An involuntary twitch blasted a bullet into a broken crate before him and then he pitched headfirst into the remnants of the crate.

A cry of derision sounded as Hilderic noticed his fate and, from the corner of his eye, he saw him move.

Without the time to raise himself, he twisted his wrists to the side and, working on instinct alone, fired through the broken wood. A cry of pain rewarded his quick action and, when he saw Hilderic, he was stumbling to the side with his left arm dangling uselessly.

Matthew batted the crate away to give him a clear shot, but before he could fire, Creighton stepped into view with his gun raised.

A gunshot ripped into Hilderic's

side, making him stagger backwards for a pace.

He stood swaying with words of defiance on his lips as he raised his gun. He never got to utter them or to fire, as two shots from Matthew and Creighton blasted into his chest. He dropped from view.

Creighton hurried through the mess on the floor to peer over the sacks where he gave a brief nod before turning to Matthew.

'Leaping headfirst off a counter,' he said, smiling, 'and shooting with deadly precision is a skill I never knew you had.'

Matthew returned the smile as he got to his feet.

'If only I'd planned to do that,' he said, 'I'd have impressed myself.'

Both men laughed before turning their attention to the one member of their group who hadn't been so lucky.

'They could have shot any one of us first,' Creighton said, standing over Tarrant's still body.

'Yeah,' Matthew said. 'Bad luck was the one situation his light-fingers couldn't deal with.'

'But at least we got the money.'

'At least *you* got it.' Matthew raised a hand when Creighton turned to him. 'I really don't want Elijah's money.'

'So what happens now, Deputy Jennings?' Creighton said with a worried croak in his voice.

'Nothing.' He patted Creighton's shoulder. 'This gunfight resolved a personal matter and so you can go. I'll stay and explain this away along with Hilderic's role in the events here.'

Creighton nodded and paced around Tarrant's body, frowning. Then, with a determined swing of the shoulders, he walked on, but stopped at the back doorway and smiled at Matthew.

'I wish you luck in your new life.'

'And the same to you.' Matthew waited until Creighton started to turn. 'But if I ever see you again — '

'I know, I know.' Creighton winked and then walked away.

Matthew waited until his footfalls had silenced. Then he put his mind to the problem of how he'd prove that Hilderic had been behind the recent events, starting with his brother's death.

Firstly, he rummaged through Hilderic's clothing. He found nothing of interest and so turned away to see if he could find where he'd been resting up.

He had yet to complete even a cursory examination of the mess in the room when a snort of contempt sounded. Elijah stepped into view beyond the window with his gun already aimed at him.

Worse, the snort had come from behind him, presumably having been made by Abraham.

'I assume,' Elijah said, 'the man I saw hightailing it out of town was Creighton.'

'It was,' Matthew said. 'Which means you won't get both of us.'

Elijah shrugged and then gestured for Matthew to drop his gun.

'He can go. All you two did is steal my money, because that's the only thing men like you can do. Once he's frittered it away, he'll go back to his old ways, whereas I can achieve so much more.'

Matthew placed his gun on the floor and then, responding to Elijah's gesture, kicked it towards him. With so much debris on the floor, the gun fetched up against a sack a few feet away.

'That's only because you never abandoned the old ways.'

Elijah's eyes narrowed, but he tried to mask his irritation by stepping over the low sill into the store. Then he peered past Matthew at the bodies.

'No matter what you think of me, I'll become the next mayor. It's a pity you won't live to see it.' Elijah removed a watch from his pocket and flicked it open. 'You have fifteen minutes to beg for your life, if you choose.'

'Your deadline means nothing to me and you won't become mayor. You didn't sign.'

'You killed Hilderic. There'll be a new deadline.'

'There won't.' Matthew set his feet wide apart, ready to leap for his gun if he saw an opening. 'Sadly for you, before I left the mayor's office, Granville signed.'

'He wouldn't dare risk the consequences,' Elijah murmured, his tone uncertain.

'There are no consequences now that Hilderic's dead. He killed my brother.'

'Except he didn't.' Elijah considered him with a sneer as he regained his usual arrogant demeanour. 'Is that what Granville told you?'

'It is,' Matthew said, although in truth he'd ignored him, 'and he had no reason to lie.'

'He did.' Elijah smirked. 'Because when we got Wilson Coney drunk, he told us that on the day Newman was killed, your father and Newman had a huge argument.'

Matthew shrugged. 'Arguments with my father aren't uncommon.'

'Maybe not, but he also said you were the first visitor to the mayor's office that day,' Elijah laughed. 'That means the only other men in the building when Newman got stabbed were Wilson and your father, and Wilson wouldn't hurt a fly.'

14

At a slow pace Matthew headed out of the store with Elijah at his side. Beneath his jacket, Elijah had pressed his gun into his ribs, while Abraham walked a few paces behind them.

Matthew walked with a stumbling gait, his shock at Elijah's revelation taking the fight out of him. He had no reason to believe that Elijah had lied, as he was a man who didn't hide behind untruths. And it could explain his father's refusal to deal with him.

At five minutes to noon, Elijah marched him into the mayor's office. Only Granville was inside.

He was sitting in the same position as he'd left him and he considered Matthew with his usual contempt that only deepened when Elijah followed him in.

Abraham moved over to stand by the

window where he could monitor the situation while Elijah left Matthew by the door to go to the desk. He considered Granville's name on the document.

'I didn't reckon you'd sign,' Elijah said, 'after we agreed not to.'

'Our deal was with Hilderic Rainhart,' Granville said, 'and I'll deal with him.'

Elijah took the document and put his name beneath Granville's.

'You don't need to. Your son dealt with him for you.' Elijah waited until Granville flicked his cold gaze past his shoulder to look at Matthew. 'So shall I cross out your name now that he's made sure the truth need never come out?'

'I could say the same to you.'

'Different people, same threats.' Elijah said, standing back from the desk and raising his gun. 'Same result.'

'Wait!' Matthew said stepping forward in fear that Elijah was about to fire. 'Elijah made an allegation about what happened to Newman. I need to hear what you've got to say about it.'

Granville didn't look at him and, although Matthew hadn't detailed what that allegation was, his downcast eyes told him everything he needed to know.

'My son was ten times the man you are,' Granville said, his tone weary, 'but he made one mistake. He thought better of you than you deserve. He refused to believe the rumour that you robbed our bank and he worked to prove it, except he worked too hard. He arrested Hilderic Rainhart and it's not surprising that Hilderic came back looking for revenge.'

'When I returned three days ago, I found Newman dying downstairs while you were in his office. I saw nobody else about that day. So I ask you: who killed him?'

'He killed himself,' Granville said. Then he sighed, presumably with relief at finally admitting the truth. 'Hilderic threatened to talk and, with your return imminent, Newman couldn't cope with the shame of arresting a man for a crime his brother carried out. He stabbed himself. But before I could get rid of the knife I'd hidden away, you found me.'

The anger that had overcome him in the store twisted Matthew's guts again. The next thing he knew he was standing beside Elijah. He slapped both hands down on the desk and leaned forward to glare at Granville.

'All this time you've poured scorn on me,' he snapped, 'and yet you've done things that are worse than I ever did.'

'I didn't,' Granville snapped back, his eyes now widening with anger. 'Your crime started this mess and forced Newman to — '

'I'm not responsible for everything that went wrong,' Matthew roared, speaking over him, his voice echoing in the room. 'I paid the price for my mistakes, so why can't you?'

'I did. I lost the only son I cared about.'

Matthew had nothing to say to that

and so, as they glared at each other, Elijah moved around the desk to consider them.

'What a pleasant homecoming this must have been for both of you,' he said. He glanced at the clock on the wall. 'It makes me wonder if I should let you carry on tearing each other apart . . . *almost.*'

The last word told Matthew what Elijah was about to do. As he was too far away to reach him, he put a hand to the nearest available weapon, which turned out to be a chair.

When Elijah swung his gun towards him, he didn't expect to get enough time to fight back, but the chair legs had yet to leave the floor when, to his surprise, Granville acted.

With an animal-like snarl, he leapt at Elijah. The desk was in the way and he went sprawling over the corner, but the action was surprising enough to make Elijah turn his gun back towards Granville.

Granville's flailing hand grasped

Elijah's jacket and dragged him down to the desk. As the two men tussled, Matthew turned away from their fight to face Abraham who was striding across the office.

His gaze was also on the fight and so Matthew hurled the chair across the room. He hadn't had enough time to aim and the chair hurtled by several feet away from its target, but it had been at head height and it made Abraham flinch away from the whirling legs.

When he jerked back, it was to face Matthew pounding across the floor. Abraham aimed his gun at him and smiled, clearly savouring the moment in which he would defeat him.

With certain defeat making his legs feel leaden, Matthew ran on. He thrust a shoulder down and ran, doubled over, in the hope that this would confuse Abraham's aim, but a gunshot blasted.

Matthew ran on for three more paces, amazed that Abraham's aim had been so poor. Then he saw the growing red mark on his opponent's chest a moment before he barrelled into him.

The two men went down and, on the floor, Matthew wasted no time in wresting the gun from Abraham's weak grip. Then, as Abraham exhaled a long and final breath, he knelt and swung round to face the desk.

Granville had shot Abraham, having taken the gun off Elijah, while Elijah lay on the floor.

'That's the first man I've ever shot,' Granville said. He swung the gun down to aim at Elijah. 'Don't force me to make it two.'

With his gaze never leaving Granville, Elijah got to his feet and stood hunched.

'I won't,' he said with a smirk. 'Instead, I'll look forward to what happens now. We'll have yet more time to enjoy a situation where neither of us can talk about what we know about the other.'

Granville didn't reply and so Matthew spoke up.

'Stand-offs can't last for ever,' he said, getting to his feet. 'Before I left the law office, I put the journal I stole from your office on Marshal Wyndham's desk. While he's been away, he'll have been working out what it means.'

Elijah's eyes flared. Then, with an angry oath, he swirled round to the door, seemingly planning to hurry from the office and reclaim the book.

He took a single pace, but then he swung back, whirling his hand. The gun he had taken off Matthew came to hand and he dragged it up from his jacket pocket.

He had yet to aim at Matthew when two shots blasted out from Granville's and Matthew's guns making him stand up straight. With a hand clutched to his chest, he glared across the office at Matthew, who limited himself to slowly shaking his head.

Elijah keeled over. He breathed once and then stilled.

'Father and son,' Matthew said, 'working together at last.'

Granville sneered, his narrowed eyes showing he was minded to restart the argument that the gunfight had interrupted and, for a terrible moment, Matthew had a vision of them facing each other in a showdown.

He opened his hand and let the gun drop to the floor and, with a gulp, as if he too had suffered the same thought, Granville threw the gun on to his desk.

'I'd have preferred you to follow my path,' Granville said, 'rather than me lowering myself to yours.'

His tone had been resigned and so Matthew glanced at the clock. It was two minutes past noon.

'What now?' he asked, heading across the office.

With a steady motion, Granville crossed out Elijah's name and then stood poised with the pen above his own name.

'I assume you'll tell Marshal Wyndham everything?'

'Of course. The full truth should come out.'

Granville nodded. He considered his name and then put the pen down without crossing through it.

'Newman died because he cared about you. I tried to follow his example.' Granville took a deep breath. 'As well as promising not to reveal what you'd done if I stole the bounty, Hilderic promised not to kill you.'

As Matthew considered that information, the door downstairs opened and footfalls came down the corridor as, presumably, Wyndham made his scheduled return. Matthew listened to him coming up the stairs and then beckoned Granville to join him in leaving.

'So,' he said, 'you've been angry with me since my return to protect me?'

'I wouldn't go that far,' Granville muttered.

They headed out of the office to find that Wyndham had arrived and that Abigail had accompanied him. Tears streaked her face as she clutched Jimmy to her side.

Matthew stepped forward while Granville

closed the door so they couldn't see the mayhem inside.

'What's wrong?' Matthew asked.

'It's Franklin,' Wyndham said, putting an arm around her shoulders. 'Earlier he was getting better, but a few minutes ago he faded away.'

'Doc Hamilton says,' Abigail murmured, fingering Jimmy's hair, 'that there was nothing he could do to save him. But Franklin did at least get to know that Jimmy was safe before . . . '

She trailed off and was unable to continue. Wyndham looked at Matthew and then at Granville for help, and this time Granville stepped forward.

'Franklin was an old and dear friend,' he said with a kindly tone as Wyndham removed his arm and passed her on to him. 'You'll always be able to depend on me.'

'Thank you,' she murmured as Wyndham offered the same sentiment.

Matthew reckoned he should keep quiet, but when she turned to the top of the stairs, she stumbled and Granville had to hold her up. Faced with her distress, silence felt wrong and he moved forward.

'If I can do anything,' he said, 'I'll help too.'

She stomped to a halt and stared straight ahead, her shoulders shaking with suppressed anger.

'I've just lost a kind and good and decent man. You're none of those things and you've already done enough damage.'

'How?'

Abigail's eyes opened wide, her angry expression showing she expected him to already know what had annoyed her, but when he said nothing, she placed a hand on Jimmy's head.

'You turned my son into a killer,' she said.

15

'It didn't happen like that,' Matthew said with as much assurance as he could muster after Abigail had delivered her breathless version of the events that morning at Snake Gorge. 'Jimmy and I were standing on the struts beneath the bridge. We kept our footing, but Lawrence Deno didn't. It's nobody's fault but his own that he fell to his death.'

With her expression still pained, Abigail looked at Jimmy, who lowered his head and mumbled something that sounded like a support of Matthew's explanation, although he then started crying.

'It is someone's fault,' Abigail said, jabbing a finger at his chest. 'It's yours. You were supposed to be looking after Jimmy.'

'I rescued him. I did everything I

could to keep him safe.'

'And taking him across a dangerous gorge along thin strips of wood to confront two hired guns was keeping him safe, was it?' Abigail glared at him, defying him to provide a retort he couldn't find. When he said nothing, distress contorted her face and she joined Jimmy in crying. She spoke between wracking sobs. 'I couldn't bare to lose him too.'

Matthew searched for a reply, but then, wisely, he said nothing and backed away for a pace.

'It'd be better for everyone,' Granville said, 'if from now on, you kept out of Abigail's and Jimmy's way.'

'Yeah,' Abigail snapped, grief fuelling her anger. 'I don't want Jimmy growing up to be like you.'

She turned away and, after pausing to gather her composure, she let Granville direct her down the stairs.

After a few uncertain steps, Jimmy extracted himself from her grip and joined Granville in helping her to negotiate the stairs. His actions made her stand up tall and they covered the remainder of the journey safely.

At the bottom of the stairs, Granville hurried on to open the door and then ushered her through. He didn't look back and neither did Abigail, but Jimmy stayed back.

He looked up the stairs and met Matthew's gaze. From his pocket, he withdrew the deputy's star he'd been given.

He fingered the star while offering him a wan smile. Matthew returned the smile until Granville came back through the doorway and put a hand on Jimmy's shoulder.

Jimmy hurriedly slipped the star back in his pocket and let Granville lead him away.

The door closed, leaving Wyndham and Matthew alone. For a minute the two men stood in silence until, with a sigh, Wyndham opened the door into the law office.

'I reckon,' he said, considering the

two bodies, 'you've got a tale to tell.'

'Yeah,' Matthew said, 'and it involves a truth that might take a while to digest — for us all.'

Wyndham nodded. 'Either way, the tension in Snake Ridge should settle down now. But I'd still like a deputy, if you're interested.'

Matthew sighed. 'I'm relieved I earned one person's respect.'

Matthew went into the office and stood looking at the mayor's desk, a desk that his father would soon occupy if the townsfolk deemed that his actions were just.

Having now had more time to consider what he'd learnt, Matthew thought they would.

Granville's crime was not to reveal that his son had taken his own life. Compared to the actions of others, this felt unimportant. And Matthew reckoned he could deal with any repercussions from the events of ten years ago now that the man who could relate those events in the worst possible light was dead.

Wyndham joined him and noted where he was looking.

'It's never easy to earn anyone's respect, but it sounded as if neither Granville or Abigail will ever be pleased to see you.'

Matthew shrugged. 'My father's mellowing.'

Wyndham raised his eyebrows in surprise. 'I've not seen any sign of that yet.'

'Since I returned, he's either told me to leave town and never return, or he's ignored me. And yet he didn't tell me to keep out of his way, only that I should keep out of Abigail's and Jimmy's way. That sounded like he's accepted I'm staying, and right now that's good enough for me.'

Wyndham slapped his back. Then he moved over to kneel beside Elijah's body.

'And Abigail?' Wyndham asked. 'If you're being that optimistic, are you going to claim you'll win her round in the end?'

Matthew knew he shouldn't torment himself, but he headed to the window and looked down into the road. The slow-moving threesome had reached the corner and someone had stopped them to offer condolences.

While Granville urged Abigail to move on, Jimmy dealt with the well-wisher. Then he hurried on to join them. After a few moments, the three people disappeared from view.

'I'll never try to do that,' he said, 'but at least she admitted that there is something I can do for her.'

He stopped hoping they'd cross over the road and let him see them again and then turned away from the window.

'Which is?'

'For the first time she told me the one thing I wanted to hear: the truth.' Matthew headed across the office to help Wyndham take the bodies away. 'She said she doesn't want Jimmy to grow up to be like me.'

Wyndham considered his tight-lipped

expression and then, as sudden understanding hit him, he darted his gaze to the window. He tipped back his hat.

'That must have been tough to hear.'

'No,' Matthew said. He crouched and gripped Elijah's shoulders. 'Because if I stay, I can make sure he doesn't.'

Wyndham put hands to Elijah's legs, but then sat back on his haunches.

'Except there's a better option,' he said. 'Stay, and make sure he does.'

THE END